HOT TIP

HOT TIP

JACK DOLPH

COACHWHIP PUBLICATIONS
Greenville, Ohio

To another and younger Jack Dolph whose devotion to the more noble forms of literature leads him to issue sharp and frequent disclaimers of these works.

Also, with, warm appreciation to Richard Hoffman—physician and mystery expert—who occasionally takes time from his career of preserving lives to cook up some especially villainous method of destroying one.

J.D.

Hot Tip, by Jack Dolph
© 2020 Coachwhip Publications edition

First published 1951
John ("Jack") Mather Dolph, 1895-1962
CoachwhipBooks.com

ISBN 1-61646-501-8
ISBN-13 978-1-61646-501-8

1

To Johnny Mallo, death had brought a last terrible indignity—a lewd mask of cherry and carmine—lips and cheeks which might have been conceived by some blowsy hag, ready for a final fling at the streets.

Only his sunken eyes were dead.

The body lay naked on the rubbing table—lean and corded with the rawhide power that had made him a great jockey. I put my hand on the flat belly. It was nastily warm.

Ralph Pack, Mallo's physician, sensed my question. He nodded toward the white reducing cabinet; open, now, showing its battery of light bulbs.

"You found him in there, Pack?"

"His wife did. She pulled him out and turned the thing off."

I called the police. If I'd heard that Johnny Mallo had died from the measles that night, I would have called the police.

It was murder, all right, but I had a hell of a time selling anybody the idea. Maybe I'd better go back a little . . .

Across the table from me, the small, lean young man ate his small, lean lamb chop, nibbled at a square of rye krisp, and swilled down about four tablespoonfuls of unsweetened tea. He stared for a moment at the piece of syrup-sopped pancake I'd left on my plate and looked up unhappily.

I said, "You must live a very interesting life."

Johnny Mallo grinned. "You know, Doc, I'm glad you reminded me. It gives me something to think about instead of food."

"What kind of weight are you making today?" The uniniti-ated would guess him around a hundred and thirty.

"Frank Latch wants me at one ten for the sixth—with or with-out one of my legs." He glanced at his water glass; ran his tongue over his lips. "It's tougher and tougher, Doc. I'm getting old."

"How old, Johnny?"

"Twenty-six. I've been riding nine years."

"You're riding too light—if you'll take a piece of medical advice on the cuff."

"Sure I am, and I pay Ralph Pack good dough to keep holler-ing it at me." He shook his dark head. "So doctors and lawyers and insurance men work too hard too. In my business you make it while you can. You've got to ride the stakes; get that 10 per cent of the purse. Like today. If I came in a pound over and got beat a head, Latch would never forgive me—"

"You riding that clumsy three-year-old of his—what's his name? Ashford?"

"That's right. Frank thinks I can hold him together." Mallo's black eyes brightened. "You know the big ones run pretty good for me once in a while, Doc."

"Like Pharaton, maybe?" The horse in question had hung Johnny on the starting gate the year before.

The boy had himself a good laugh. "Is that nice? I invite you to an expensive breakfast and you throw that harpoon into me!"

"Incidentally, Johnny, why *did* you invite me to breakfast after neglecting me for six months? Got something on your mind?"

"Yeah." He looked at his watch. "Can you drive out to the track with me?"

As a matter of form I ran down my list of nothing to do before I accepted. Broadway was noisy and dirty and hot. Of course it would be noisy and dirty and hot at the track, too, but that's different. I followed Mallo to his car with the school's-out feeling I always have when I head for the races.

Until we got out of the Midtown Tunnel, Johnny was ex-pertly busy with traffic and we didn't say much. As he hit the Boulevard, the little man lit a cigarette.

"You know my kid brother, Doc? Mickey?"

"Only by reputation."

"Reputation?" There was an edge in Mallo's voice.

"Isn't he supposed to be the top apprentice rider of the season?"

"Yeah." He spurred the big Buick and snarled around a dozen cars. "Mick's supposed to be a lot of things he isn't."

"Has he got himself into trouble?" Lord knows there's plenty of it around the horses if a boy looks for it—he either walks the line or he walks the streets.

"I don't know, Doc. Maybe. He's asking for it."

"How?"

"You know Huck Trask?"

"Not well. He speaks to me for some reason." The hustling publisher of *Huck's Hot Horses* wasn't exactly my brand of boon companion, but I'd never heard anything very unpleasant about him. "I know his tip sheet, of course. Where does he fit in?"

"Trask hates my guts—for a lot of reasons. He's been trying to make it tough for me for years. Now he and his wife have practically taken the kid over. Mick's with them all the time, and when I tell him how bad it looks he won't listen to me."

"It wouldn't look good, that's sure." Though a race rider seldom has information that's worth a dime, most people think he has. Hanging out with a professional tipster would get quick attention from the old gentlemen in the front office. "Have you any reason to think Trask is trying to cook up a deal of some sort?"

"Yes." Mallo threw his hat into the back seat without taking his eyes off the road. "I've got proof. For a couple of months now I've suspected Trask would try to pull something with the kid. Right after Jamaica closed in the spring, Mick stopped paying on his insurance and started getting closemouthed about money. From that time on . . ."

"You were taking care of his affairs?"

"I always have. I was his legal guardian for several years. We've got identical insurance policies with each other as beneficiaries. It's a swell way to build an estate, and we put all our savings into it—until sometime in May. Then last night I found this." Johnny dug into his pocket and fumbled with a wallet, produced a piece of paper, and handed it to me.

It was a conventional bookmaker's betting slip—two hundred dollars to win on Nautilus in the fourth race that day. It was made out for "Mr. O.K." I said, "I don't get it."

Mallo snapped his cigarette out the window. "You haven't seen the entries then. Mickey's riding Agency Man in the fourth—a short-priced favorite."

A jockey, if he's old enough to bet at all, may wager on his own mount. Caught betting on any other horse in the race, he might as well hang up his tack and look for a job in a riding academy. He's through with racing. The slip could have meant anything from a stupid-kid idea to a national coup involving serious money. I said, "That could be very nasty. I wonder how much Trask has going—Trask and maybe a string of his customers."

"Whatever it is, they'll lose it, Doc. That's why I called you this morning—I wanted somebody to know about it, and you're the only person I could think of that might understand. Mick won't be riding the fourth race."

"Does he know that yet?"

"Not yet." Johnny grinned stiffly.

"By tomorrow you'll be a strictly unpopular guy in certain quarters, I suspect." Sure-thing gamblers are extremely bad losers. "You won't turn the boy in to the stewards, will you?"

"Not if I can help it." We pulled off into the side road that leads to the stable area. "The publicity would be damned bad for me too."

"How'd you happen to get hold of the betting slip? I wouldn't think he'd have left it lying around."

"He didn't. When I got home last night, Mick and my wife were having sandwiches. The kid doesn't have to watch his weight yet. I sat out in the kitchen with them for a while, and then the phone rang. It was Trask asking for Mickey. I gave Trask hell and hung up in his face. Mick was wild, said he had important business with Trask and tried to grab the phone away. I wouldn't let him use it, so he took a poke at me."

"And the brawl was on!"

"You can say *that* again! We bounced around the place and ended up in the kitchen with Lorry hollering murder." Mallo frowned. "We damned near had one at that. The bread knife was on the table, and Mick went for it." The little man took an amazingly big hand off the wheel and pulled up his coat sleeve. His forearm was bandaged. "I got cut taking it away from him, and it made me mad. I hit him a couple of times and threw him out of the apartment."

"How did you get the betting slip while all that was going on?"

"He'd dropped his pocketbook. I was looking through it when he came back and pounded on the door. I kept the slip and chucked the wallet under a chair, then let him in to look for it."

As we pulled into the horsemen's parking space, I noticed a cream-colored convertible ahead of us and recognized Trask. Young Mallo was with him. They were talking intently for some time before they climbed out of the car. Johnny said, "There they are now. We might as well walk over to the office."

We leaned on the rail in front of the riders' quarters and watched them split up—Trask heading toward the clubhouse and Mickey approaching us with some urgency. A program butcher was untying his day's supply, and I went over and bought one. I stood away from Johnny when I went back, leaned on the rail and studied the entries. I heard Mickey's voice, expressionless and hard.

"I left something at your place last night. I want it."

"You got it. Or did you leave something besides your wallet?"

"Goddamn you, don't give me that! You took something out of it, and I want it back!"

I said, "Hello, Mickey."

He turned, the fury still in his eyes. "You're Doc Connor, aren't you??

"That's right. I'm glad to know you." I stuck out my hand, and the boy gave me a limp wet paw. "You lose something, Mickey?"

He was some time getting the anger off his face. "It wasn't very important, only this jerk can't keep his nose out of other people's business. You going to be around for the races, Doc?"

"Yes. How about marking my program for me?"

"Me pick horses for you? That'll be the day! If you didn't have a sweet bet going, you probably wouldn't be out here. What do you like?"

I conjured a sickening chuckle, which reminded me of everybody I like the least. "What do you think of that, Johnny? The boy who's riding the best bet of the day asks me what I like!" Neither of them said anything. "Agency Man! That's the one. He'll be a short price, but I prefer 'em that way."

Mickey looked up at me, and down again. "Yeah. He could win it, all right." Then he scuffed off toward the jock house.

Johnny ground out a laugh. "Well, Doc?"

"What do you want me to do?"

"I don't know. Maybe you could get some place with the kid—if you felt like it. He thinks you're O.K."

"So? How come?"

"Well . . . Hell, Doc, he's got you pegged for one of the aces—the bright boys."

"No visible means of support."

Mallo flushed a little. "It's none of my business, of course. You get around with all the best people—the sporting crowd, show folks. Mick takes it for granted you do it the easy way."

"And what do *you* think, Johnny?"

"Why . . . I don't know, Doc. I hear you take care of a lot of sick people around Forty-eighth Street and never send out any bills. You don't do that playing the horses."

"That's right. I don't. I'll have a talk with the boy if you want."

"Thanks a lot." He looked over his shoulder at the jock-house door. "I guess I'd better go in and have a talk with him myself. See you maybe tomorrow?"

"Right. I'll call you."

I watched him walk off and burned a little, as I always do when my sins come home to roost. There are times when my uselessness won't stay laughed off. My carefully planned medical college to army to general practice program had bogged down somewhere in the South Pacific, and I'd never quite gotten back to work.

Rugged old Uncle Will Connor had done for me what he'd liked to have done for my father—the old Doc. Unk had been richly successful in a lifetime of making bricks without straw, while his favorite brother had been richly rewarded, in a lifetime of country practice, by making friends without money. When I came back from the service, I found I'd been left a substantial annuity.

So far I'd been able to withstand the gentle criticism of my two best friends—the beautiful Katie Storm and Lieutenant Edward Quinn Marsh of the New York Police Department. But a kid like Mickey Mallo . . .

I took a *Racing Form* up to the clubhouse and sat around for three quarters of an hour trying to figure out horses that could beat the winners—an occupational disease with horse players.

At one o'clock the public-address system cleared its throat and started barking the program changes. Among them: ". . . and in the fourth race, number nine—Agency Man—a change of jockeys. The jockey on number nine—H. Fenton—H. Fenton. In the fifth race . . ."

I wondered how much—and just what—persuasion Johnny had used to make Mickey call off the deal. Immediately after the announcement I caught a glimpse of Huck Trask hurrying out of the clubhouse, his face grim. I didn't see him again.

The afternoon turned out to be pleasant and profitable. My one bet—a five-dollar venture on Ashwick—rewarded me with forty-five dollars and eighty cents as Johnny Mallo brought the big colt from last place on the back-stretch to come booming home, three long-striding lengths on top.

The fourth race, without benefit of Mickey or a bet from me, went according to the suddenly revised script. H. Fenton, disinterested in the fate of Nautilus, romped in with Agency Man, as the odds had suggested he might.

By the last race I had learned that Mickey had canceled all four of his riding engagements. He'd not only lost his two hundred dollars but his afternoon's work with it.

I headed for the exit wondering again how much Huck Trask and possibly others had dropped on the race. On the way out I bought an evening paper and learned that Johnny Mallo was booked to ride something call Finney in the third on Saturday—at one hundred and eleven pounds.

2

I rode a cab back that evening, because that is also an occupational disease with winning horse players and because I had a date with the peerless Katie Storm. From Monday through Friday her beautiful Irish nose is pressed to the microphone, but on Friday nights she allows herself a little ladylike howling. Katie's "Recipes-in-Rhythm" program is a daily favorite with the girls who go for gay kitchens and such things as capers in their cooking.

By three-thirty in the morning we had done a fair kind of a country job on the town and a rather complete one on my ill-gotten dough. Over ritual scrambled eggs and a kipper, Katie ticked off the plans for her annual visit to the old homestead in Ohio—a sort of working vacation, during which she does her show from her mother's kitchen.

The mama-teaches-famous-daughter gimmick is meringue for the customers, but it's a headache for both the network and me. The engineers hate it because there's a dismal echo in the Storm kitchen, and I, because there's always a dismaller one in the Connor breast.

Katie was sweetly serious as we stood in front of her apartment building. "Well . . . this is it, Jimmy darling. I'm on my way at eleven-thirty. Are you going to miss me?"

"Terribly!" I think I said it twice. It looks different when you write it down.

She smiled warmly, the street light touching the curve of her cheek. "I've got a kind of . . . drooly idea . . ."

If I'd been in my right mind, I'd have recognized the back-door approach. Katie doesn't have drooly ideas. As it was, I said, "Tell me about it."

"Do you remember when you were—oh, maybe seventeen—and somebody you loved very much was going away, and you wanted them to *leave* something with you to keep for them? Something terribly personal?"

"Of course I do, darling. We've always had a little of the high-school feeling too. Haven't we?"

She nodded gravely. "Yes. We have, somehow." She touched my face gently. "Would you think it was silly if I did that? Left something for you to—watch over?"

"Don't you *know* I wouldn't think it was silly? I'd love it."

"And you'd—*cherish* it?"

"Every waking moment. What would it be? Tell me!"

"Sauki-no-no! Isn't that *sweet?*"

"Never!" I thrust the woman from me. My blood ran cold. Sauki-no-no is Katie's highly vocal and extremely female Siamese cat., She is strictly a Beekman Place cat and wants no part of the denizens of my end of town. I have been expertly snubbed in my life, but never with the frigid hauteur I get from Sauki-no-no's cold blue eyes.

"I'll have nothing to do with the damned cat! This is a con game—a racket! You're trying to save a buck a day. Send her to the Sauki Cattery like you always do. I wouldn't—"

"James Connor, sometimes I think that secretly—*secretly,* mind you—you *dislike* animals!"

"I do not dislike animals. I love animals. It's simply that—"

From that point on the discussion proceeded in orderly fashion to the point where, as I kissed Katie good-by, I did so over a large cat carrier, a bedpan or something, two pounds of frozen horse meat, and endless bottles of assorted vitamins.

I made it to a cab, and the driver helped load us into my apartment—adding gratuitous advice garnered from the days when his wife had had a cat. I fixed myself a bracing Old Forester and water and started to undress. My lodger busied herself with a detailed inspection of the premises until I got down to my underclothes. Then she sat down and inspected me. My shorts are admittedly on the loud side, but it didn't seem an occasion for staring.

"What's the matter? Don't you like 'em?"

"Wow!"

It was distinct, bawdy, and final. I was meditating bitterly on the soul-rotting conservatism of East-Siders in general when the telephone rang.

"Dr. Connor?"

I said yes, wondering who would be calling me at four-twenty in the morning.

"This is Ralph Pack. I don't know whether you remember me. I'm a physician."

"Of course. What can I do for you, Doctor?"

"Frankly, I don't exactly know. A patient of mine has died under unusual—most unusual—circumstances." The man sounded pretty well disturbed. "I'd like professional confirmation of my findings. If you would be good enough to—"

"Why did you call me? I'm not in regular practice."

"You were a friend of Mallo's and I thought—"

"*Which* Mallo?"

"Johnny."

"What's the address? I'll be right over."

I wrote down the number and jumped into my clothes. *Johnny* Mallo! The wrong one. If somebody had killed Mickey that night, I could have understood it. On the other hand, it was Johnny who had upset the deal.

By four-forty I was at the door of Johnny's apartment, shaking hands with a youngish, well-built man who gave me the you-were-so-good-to-come business and hustled me into the living room.

"I think when you've seen this situation, Dr. Connor, you'll understand why I called you. I've seen nothing like it before." He peered at me for a moment, and damned if he didn't start blushing. "You—you *are* licensed to practice in New York State, aren't you?"

"Of course. I just don't do much of it."

"Yes. I see." The guy looked a little surprised. "Good! I'll just take you back myself. I've given Mrs. Mallo a sedative."

He took off down a narrow hall that led to the rear of the apartment. It was bounded on the left by a solid wall but sprouted rooms along the right. Small sounds through one of the closed doors indicated Mrs. Mallo's bedroom.

At the end of the hall a partition set off what looked, at first glance, like a small surgery—white enameled walls, black linoleum floor, and a blazing light overhead. In the center of the floor stood a boxlike sweat cabinet. Its door was open, showing a towel-covered chair with its legs in several inches of water—evidently a tiled footbath. A tumbler switch on the inside wall of the cabinet operated the heat-producing lights. It was off.

Elsewhere in the room were a glass-enclosed shower, a small sink, a good sliding-weight scale, and a rubbing table on which lay the body of Johnny Mallo.

Pack told me tersely of what he'd found on arrival. Then he added, "Dehydration, of course." He lit a cigarette and paced around the room while I took in the scene.

It was dehydration all right, but dehydration and *what?* Johnny was as familiar with reducing baths as you are with your hairbrush. I turned to Pack.

"Why didn't he climb out?"

"I don't know—lost consciousness, I guess. He had a good deal of trouble with his weight—reduced a lot. I'd warned him—"

"Of what? Of this?"

Pack bristled a little. "Naturally not! Of his general condition. The man was in a dehydrated state most of the time. He didn't eat properly; insisted on—"

"I know. He told me yesterday. Did you know Mallo well?"

"Intimately. We've been friends for several years."

"Do you play the races?"

The guy blew. "What the hell are you talking about?"

"Never mind. It was simply a social question—I was thinking of something else."

"This is hardly a social call, Connor. Suppose we think about the problem at hand."

"All right. How about his heart?"

"Completely sound. I have his ECG's at the office." Pack started pacing again. I asked him how long he thought Mallo had been dead. He stopped in front of me and stared.

"Look, Connor, suppose I tell you the facts and then *you* tell *me* how long he's been dead. Here they are." He resumed his constitutional. "Mrs. Mallo says she went to bed about ten o'clock and that Johnny was on his way to this room. He's usually not more than an hour or so at the most, although he would occasionally roll up in a blanket and lie on the rubbing table for a while after his sweat. Mrs. Mallo's never had any reason to worry about his reducing, so she read for half an hour or so and went to sleep."

"Was the outside door locked?"

He looked surprised. "How the hell would I know if it was locked?"

"I thought you might have noticed when Mrs. Mallo let you in."

"I didn't. What's the difference? You trying to make a crime out of this?"

"Not necessarily. Go on with the story."

"Lorry—that's Mrs. Mallo—woke up shortly after three o'clock and missed her husband. She thought he might have fallen asleep on the table and would take cold. He was still in the cabinet when she found him—with all the heat on. He'd apparently been in it for something more than five hours. At three forty-five the temperature of the body was beyond the capacity of a clinical thermometer."

Pack pulled up in front of me and peered. "Have you got any answers, Doctor?"

"No." I prowled around the room. There was something under the table that looked like an alarm clock—an exposure timer. They're used in X-ray laboratories, darkrooms, beauty parlors—any place where you want to time something roughly. You set the alarm for X minutes from now and in X minutes the thing tells you you're through. It hadn't told Johnny Mallo he was through though. The alarm had been set for thirty-five minutes and had run down.

I heard Pack step on the scale platform and said, "Hold it!"

"What's the matter?"

"Don't touch the adjustment. Let's see what he weighed before he went into the cabinet."

"Oh?" He climbed down and looked puzzled in a disinterested way. "What would that tell us?"

"I know what he weighed yesterday. The scale could show whether he'd eaten or if, possibly, he'd been out of the bath and gone back." I looked at the sliding weight, but it had apparently been shoved aside since Mallo had used it—a good two inches past any adjustment that would concern Johnny. "It's been kicked around. Anyway, it was a good idea. Go ahead and weigh yourself."

Pack turned away from the scale. "Why worry about what he weighed? He probably weighs ninety pounds now. Hell, Connor! The man's dead!" The physician was irritated. "Insufficient fluids, no food, violent exertion every day—a rotten life!"

"A rotten death, if you ask me. You going to certify it?"

"Why not?" He stuck his chin out.

"You know perfectly well that somebody could have slugged the man and shoved him into the box." I stuck my own chin out some.

"I never thought of violence in connection with the accident. There wouldn't be any reason for—"

"Godammit, Pack, there's every reason to think of violence in connection with it! This man may have cost a group of professional gamblers a hell of a lot of money yesterday!" The bandage from Johnny's forearm lay on the floor. "I see you examined the knife wound."

"Knife wound? I looked at the cut on his arm. You talk as if somebody had—inflicted it." He was defensive as a bull pup.

"Somebody did." I must have been barking because he put up his hand in mild protest "I'm sorry, Pack, I liked the boy and he was apparently in a lot of trouble. Shall we call the police?"

"I suppose so—if you insist."

We went back to the living room and I called Eddie Marsh at his place. He grumbled quite a lot—claimed I had bourbon on my breath—and finally agreed to come over. As I hung up I heard Pack murmur, "I hope the sedation has helped, Lorry."

"It has—thank you, Ralph. I am feeling very much better."

She was looking very much better too. Poor Johnny had really left himself a relict. I'd seen her around a few times—always thought she looked like a Fourth-of-July flag—red hair, milk-white skin, and intensely blue eyes. La Mallo was jockey-wife size with a bouncy, rounded little figure that promised some extra roundness for the years to come. It also promised things that would make a man forget the years to come—maybe a man like Pack. She greeted me pleasantly, and we exchanged such amenities as you can dig up on that sort of occasion. After a while Pack broke in with a tight voice. "Dr. Connor feels that it would be advisable to report the accident to the police. He has called someone."

"The police?" Lorry put her handkerchief to her mouth and sat down suddenly in a big chair. She looked very small. "Why would it be necessary to discuss it with the police, Doc?"

"Simply because it's the law."

"I don't understand. Nobody would have . . . I mean . . ." The words piled up in her throat. She started to cry.

"I'm sorry, Lorry. Fatal accidents have to be reported to the authorities. I'm sure Dr. Pack understands that. You see, they'll want to make certain that Johnny didn't slip in the shower and hurt his head or—anything like that."

We had a bad quarter hour until Eddie Marsh turned up. Lorry Mallo was terribly confused, and, for some reason of her own, terribly frightened.

I did manage to assure myself during that period, however, that she knew nothing whatever of the real reason for her husband's quarrel with his brother. I observed, also, that the family physician was unusually attentive.

3

Marsh had been mildly interested, noncommittal, and especially uncommunicative. He'd sent for a couple of his men, and they'd gone over the place, physically, leaving the circumstantial work for him. When they'd taken Johnny away and sealed up the room, we went back to my place in full daylight.

In the kitchen, Eddie drank coffee and watched Sauki-no-no foul up my legs while I was trying to thaw out her breakfast. I said, "Well, what do you think?"

He slid down in his chair and pushed a tremendous pair of black shoes halfway across the room. "Am I supposed to think?"

"I haven't looked it up in the police handbook, but it might be a hell of an idea."

"It doesn't say I must do autopsies on every accident case, and it specifically says I mustn't run around accusing people of crimes they didn't commit. How about some more coffee?"

"I'm not asking you to accuse anybody." I filled his cup.

"A very good thing too. I'm not going to accuse anybody." I never get used to his four spoonfuls of sugar. "Thanks."

"Coffee good?"

"Excellent!" He took a delicate sip with his little finger stuck out. "You may have used just a trifle—just a pinch—too much curry in it. Do you ever wash that pot?"

I gave the cat her meat. She hove into it with no complaints. Eddie looked out the window. I said, "Maybe you did some thinking about Lorry Mallo—"

"Very tasty!"

"Don't leer. It makes you look subnormal."

"Doc, there's a woman that's just too much responsibility for one man." Marsh is a determined bachelor and argues in favor of the condition. "She's the kind you don't lose track of during office hours."

"Do you suppose Johnny lost track of her during office hours?"

"Maybe. I wouldn't go too far with any of that though. It doesn't look like much to me—unless, of course, they find Mallo with a bellyful of arsenic or something. If he'd had a shive in his ribs, I'd have run out to the track this afternoon at the public expense, and, when I'd won a couple of bets, pulled young Mallo off a horse." Eddie got up and stretched tiredly. "I've got to go. I'll call you when the lab reports come back."

"Want to use my razor?"

"Thanks. I've got one at the office." He drank the last of his coffee. "Why don't you run down Huck Trask today and see what he's got to offer?"

"Well I'll be damned! Do I detect a grain of curiosity?"

"There's nothing in the handbook says I can't be curious—on my own time. See you later, Doc. Thanks for the Java."

I took a shower and changed my clothes; killed time one way and another until straight up to nine o'clock. I figured Trask would be in his office by then. He had to distribute *Huck's Hot Horses* by eleven, and Saturday was a big day.

I dug up the phone book. Trasea, Trasgreve, Trash Disposal Corp., Trask, H. J., pub. The address was one of those midtown rabbit warrens where you pay a month at a time, in advance, and don't nail anything down. I decided against calling him, got my hat, and set out.

The door said "Trask Publications." I went in, and pulled up fast almost in the lap of a production number with tow hair and a very red dress. She was in a cubicle, cut out of the single office, which contained, otherwise, a typewriter desk, a filing cabinet, and no air. Somewhere behind her I could hear a chair squeak, suggesting the boss was penned up inside.

"Trask around?"

Her eyes calmly did everything but take my fingerprints. "I'm not sure. Who shall I say is calling?"

"Doc Connor."

"Oh!" Flattering. "I'll see if he's in." She got up.

"If he isn't, he's just jumped out the window."

The blonde lifted her head and smiled—with teeth. "Perhaps he has, Doctor. He used to do it often when we were down on the sixth floor." She opened the inner door and didn't bother to close it. "Do you want to talk to a comic by the name of Doc Connor?"

Trask laughed. "Come in, Doc. This is my wife, Eve. You must have needled her. She gets that way."

"I'll know better next time. Hello, Eve."

She stuck out a big, competent hand and grabbed mine like she was fixing to Indian-rassle. "Hello, Doc. You do all right. The window bit was swell—didn't think I'd be able to top it for a minute."

The man in the big chair said, "O.K., Mama, back to your cage. You can kid with the company later."

Mama smiled at me. "Perhaps you'll drop by the desk on the way out."

As the door closed Trask said, "Sit down. What can I do for you? I take it for granted you don't want a horse."

"I just threw one away, thanks. I want some information— not about horses."

"About jockeys, maybe?" He didn't smile.

"That's right. How'd you guess?"

"I saw you talking to Johnny Mallo yesterday at the track." Trask got a box of bad cigars out of the desk and offered me one which I declined hurriedly. "Johnny makes a point of raising a squawk because I'm friendly with his young brother. I figured he must have been crying to you." Business of lighting the cigar.

"He was."

"To hell with him. Am I a pariah just because I publish a handicapping service?"

"Johnny's dead." I simply put it on the line and let it lie. Trask's face froze. He held it a moment, then deliberately put his cigar down on the ash tray.

"How?"

"In his reducing cabinet—at home." I went over it for him without voicing any opinions or referring to the police. I made no mention whatever of Friday afternoon's events. When I'd finished, he sat without speaking. The typewriter outside was quiet. Finally he said, "That will be a rough deal for Mickey. It's too bad."

"Why Mickey, especially?"

"The boys haven't been getting along. They had a hell of a brawl in the jock house yesterday. Mick had to cancel his mounts for the day."

"Is that why he canceled his mounts?"

"Hell! The kid was all marked up—one of his eyes half closed. He couldn't have ridden."

"That's not the way I heard it, Trask." I made it hard.

"What do you mean?"

"Has Eddie Marsh asked you any questions yet?"

Trask frowned; dug his cigar out of the ash tray. "Why would Marsh want to ask me questions?"

I heard the office door open, and then Eve walked up to us. "This is getting past the comedy stage, Doc. I'm sitting in." She talked as though she had a gun in her hand. "Go ahead. Why would Eddie Marsh want to ask Huck questions?"

"You heard that Johnny's dead?" I was stalling for time.

"I'm not deaf—nor as dumb as I look. Let's hear the rest."

I made up my mind to take it easy, for the time being. "The police are interested in knowing why a man who had recently made some bad enemies should suddenly die—doing something he'd done without incident for years. They are curious to know if any outside influence might have—contributed."

Trask was taut as an E string. He walked over and looked out the window. Eve said, "Outside influence—like what?"

"Like a blow on the head, for instance, or poison. They'll do an autopsy, of course."

The blonde was thoughtful—hesitated—asked, "You say Johnny had recently made some bad enemies. What did you mean by that?"

Trask turned from the window. "He means Mickey." She looked up at her husband. "I don't think he does."

I wanted to bay like a hound. "Who do you think I mean, Eve?"

"You didn't come over here to play games, Doc. What do you want of us?"

"For one thing, I want to find out if either of you know what was on a piece of paper Mickey lost out of his wallet—something he accused Johnny of stealing from him. It must have been important to him. If Johnny had it, the cops will get it. Then they'll ask questions."

Trask said, "I'm on pretty good terms with young Mallo, but I've managed to keep my hands out of his wallet."

"Have you?"

"Don't get cute, Connor. Save your gags for Eve—I don't go for them." He came back from the window and sat at the desk again.

"There are quite a lot of things in connection with Johnny's death you won't go for, Trask."

"Are you trying to suggest I had something to do with it?" The skin tightened across his face; his ears flattened to his head.

"I am trying to get you to answer a simple question. Do you know what was on that paper?"

From beside me I heard Eve say, very quietly, "Do you, Doc?"

You could have counted your fingers while we held the pose. I should have expected the question, but it was a quick turn.

Then I said, "Yes. I know."

I pegged the Trasks up a notch when neither of them inquired why I was asking them, if I knew. Neither of them said anything. I picked up my hat, and the woman went back to her desk. Trask didn't move while we heard her close the door and rattle her chair outside. Then he made a small gesture with his hand.

"So that's the way it's going to be, Doc?"

"What way?"

"Public action against Mickey, with the—piece of paper as the People's Exhibit number one. The kid loses his license to ride, and others lose—other things—by implication." He picked up a pencil and started doodling on a pad. "Is that the way it's going to be, Doc?"

"Can you think of any reason why it shouldn't?" I had no intention of letting Trask know I hadn't told Eddie Marsh about the betting tab—simply suggested the boy might have been involved in some sort of a deal.

The guy didn't look up from his scribbling. "Yes. I can think of several—the principal one being that I don't want to be put out of business through no fault of my own."

"That's strictly for the end book, Trask. I'm wasting my time. You could bleat your innocence from now on—and you probably will—but you still had a piece of the Nautilus deal."

He chucked his pencil aside, took his hand off the doodling. A musical staff and notes. The "Prisoner's Song," maybe. When he spoke, his voice was restrained, narrative. "I print a card, Connor, a pretty good one. It's a legal operation and it makes me a fair living. When I get enough capital, I want to handle a few riders—I was a jockey's agent once before. Mickey would have come with me by now, except for his brother."

His life story, but with music! "Why all this, Huck?"

He snapped out of his reflective mood. "Because if you cost me my reputation on account of some punk kid who tried to win a few cheap dollars, I'll slap a defamation action on you that'll cook you. Is that plain?"

"How did you know Mickey tried to win a few cheap dollars, as you put it?" I thought I had something.

"Because he crawled to me last night with the story. Johnny cuffed the hell out of him in the jock house and made him cancel his mounts on threat of exposure." Trask stood up suddenly. "I think that about winds us up, Doc."

I didn't like the way it stood. The only thing that would account for his confidence was the possibility that either he or Mickey had recovered the tab. I'd better have a look for it. I said, "One thing more, Trask—Johnny said you hated his guts—for several reasons. Why was that?"

"Because it's quite true, although he was probably talking more about his own feelings than mine. You see, I married the only real woman he'd ever known in his nasty, selfish life." The man looked very formidable. "Now I'd like to get back to my work."

There didn't seem to be anything to say, so I went out through Eve's cubbyhole—took, a chance on playing straight for her again. She didn't look up until I spoke.

"You suggested I drop by on my way out—"

She gave me those nice white teeth again. "Under the circumstances, don't you think it would have been more thoughtful of you to drop out the back way?"

4

I squelched a violent, desire to see Katie off and stopped by Rosie's for a waffle. Katie has very set ideas about parting wavings and mutterings. She also has ideas about my mixing up with murders. In a little more than three years' association with Eddie Marsh I'd involved myself in several pretty sensational cases, with attendant publicity that dimmed Katie's dreams of a bronze sign and an East Side practice.

Sooner or later I'd lose my apprentice allowance and have to turn criminologist or give up playing cops 'n robbers entirely. The Mallo-Trask thing was bound to be especially unpleasant. I went home filled with high resolve to stay out of it.

The morning was already getting sticky, and a shower provided only momentary relief. Sauki-no-no had nothing to say about my taste in shorts, or anything else, for that matter. She'd found the Forty-eighth Street window and was pressed up against the screen watching a large, dirty male cat—a casual acquaintance of mine—hustle his breakfast at the back door of a restaurant across the way.

She didn't exactly yoo-hoo or anything, but I got the impression that she had developed more than a passing interest in the mores of Broadway felinity.

Somebody downstairs leaned on the buzzer—the office side which my friends never use. I went through to my desk and picked up the intercom. It was Mickey Mallo.

"Huck Trask said you want to see me."

"Maybe I do. Come on up. I'll leave the office door open."

I raised the window and took the door off the latch. On Tuesday and Thursday mornings the place is S.R.O. with local characters. The rest of the week it just sits and accumulates mail from pharmaceutical houses.

By the time I'd jumped into a pair of slacks and a cool shirt, the boy was wandering, around the reception room with his hat on, looking at my horse pictures. He stood in front of the enlargement which is my pride and joy.

"Them jumping riders sure get it! The guy that took that spill got himself hurt plenty."

"Not a scratch, Mick, but I saw eight bellies go over my head."

"That was you, eh? You ride a lot when you were a kid?"

"Some. Hunt meetings on the Coast mostly." I opened the office door. "Let's go in and sit down."

"Why not?"

I got behind the desk and Mickey sat in the confessional, earnestly trying to read a letter inviting me to prescribe something called Amperol. I led off, "I'm sorry about Johnny, kid."

"Yeah. It was too bad about Johnny."

"I suppose Lorry called you about it this morning."

"She said you called the cops. What was that for?"

His face was expressionless, partly because a large area of it was neatly painted with Covermark and his left eye was only a dull gleam between puffy lids. Johnny must have really worked him over,

"I called the cops because you're supposed to in that kind of an accident, Mick."

"Yeah? Why?"

"Oh . . . insurance, for one thing. Johnny probably had some insurance, didn't he?"

"Maybe he did. What about it? They've got to pay off, don't they?" I thought of the brothers' identical policies and wondered how much Mickey stood to win—or lose.

"There's a pretty good chance they won't have to pay off at all—just the amount of the premiums."

The young beneficiary was seriously disturbed. "You're nuts! They've got to pay off double on account of double—whaddy-acallit."

"You been reading your policy this morning?"

"I remember what the guy said. The only kind of accident you don't get paid on is if you get knocked off on the track." He said it loud enough to drown out his doubts.

"Maybe the man said that, Mick, but I'll lay you a little bet that the policy doesn't. I think you'll find that the company will claim exemption from payment in accidents suffered—as they would probably put it—while 'pursuing his hazardous occupation.' You'd have a hell of a time proving that severe weight reduction—against professional advice and for the purposes of racing—isn't a part of that occupation."

"I don't believe it." He frowned on his less edematous side. "Why, that would leave Lorry—" He hesitated, as if he were counting on his fingers.

"You're quite right. That would leave Lorry in something of a spot." I wanted to spell it out for him so he could carry it back to her. "If Johnny had been struck on the head or forced, in any way, to stay in the sweatbox longer than he should have, Lorry would receive double the face of the policy. But she'd have to prove it herself. The insurance people certainly wouldn't help any."

He was quite a while getting around to the idea that his sister-in-law needed to catch herself a murderer. When he did, he didn't like any part of it. "Do the cops think maybe somebody—did something to Johnny? Hit him or something?"

"They'll know more about it after the autopsy. By tonight, probably. They can tell if there's a skull fracture or poison—almost any sort of force or drug that might have been used on him."

"Could he—" The kid squirmed some. "I guess you'll find out that we had a fight at the track yesterday."

"I knew that, Mickey. If it's any satisfaction to you, I doubt if any blow you struck Johnny at noon yesterday would have caused his death."

"I'm sure glad of that. A guy wouldn't like to get accused of killing his brother!"

"No. Although they'll probably ask you why you tried to kill him on Thursday night."

"Tried to kill him! Who tried to kill him?"

"You. With a butcher knife. Lorry saw it all."

"*Lorry* never told you that!" Noble as a library lion. "She wouldn't tell anything that would go against me."

"Don't be too sure, kid. There's money involved—quite a lot, probably. Lorry can't afford to be too generous." He gave this some attention and didn't look too happy about it. Then I added, "She probably knows about the Nautilus deal, too, doesn't she?"

He tried two or three ideas that never got farther than an open mouth. His gum showed, kept showing until I said, "Huck Trask talked, Mickey."

"All right. Let him talk some more. I'm through." He stood up and started for the door, I let him get most of the way.

"I don't know where you got the idea you could beat the races by taking short cuts, Mallo, but you'd better not accept any mounts until you've changed your attitude."

He whirled around. "Who says so?"

"I say so. I don't go for bets like that."

"Out of you that's a laugh." There it was. I did a fast burn. Lost my control and started throwing them high and inside.

"Listen, you smart punk, and get this straight. If your name comes up in the entries until I let you ride again, I'll have you set down for life—back gate and front."

He made a loud, vulgar sound—often attributed to our good neighbors to the north. I probably would have chased him down the hall if the telephone hadn't rung. It was Eddie Marsh, and could I come over to the Precinct right away—he had news for me. I did the six blocks in something less than par for the course.

He was in a disinfectant-laden back office and looking very pleased with himself. "Close the door, mastermind, I've got bad news for you."

"Like what?" I sat down.

"Like you've got no murder."

"Who told you?"

"Experts, my friend."

"And just which experts make this pronouncement?"

"None other, I'll have you know, than the eminent Dr. Crane—assisted by Dr. Penfield and Yalt. That was the first team. On the junior varsity were such luminaries as Dr. Het-lick, from the insurance company, your friend Pack, and a shyster named Sam Fenner. Somebody should have sold tickets."

Anyway, that took the pressure off. "Don't tell me Storky Crane actually *performed* an autopsy!"

"The great man rose up early in the morning and did it—with his own little hatchet."

"Your hyperbole is—indelicate."

"The post-mortem was no bargain in that department either."

"I'll bet Storky held forth."

"But for more than an hour. He had a field day droning out what goes with dehydration. Hell! I always thought it was what the Army does to vegetables." Marsh sat back and licked his chops over my obvious disappointment.

"Did anybody bother to find out if he'd been hit over the head?"

"Yes indeed! Thorough is the name for Storky. Your young man had not been hit over the head hard enough to make him sleep through that timer alarm. No hemorrhage, no hypodermic punctures, not the slightest indication that anything had been administered to him, no trace of drugs—"

"How about bruises around the face and head? He had a fight yesterday afternoon, you know."

"Right! I brought that up before my superiors and got slapped down."

"How?"

"Thus." Eddie hauled out his old black notebook. "I jotted it down—if you can call this sort of thing jotting. Storky says—wait a minute—Storky says that 'in the absence of collateral indicia, the facial contusions are, for the purposes of this investigation, negligible.' How do you like them apples?"

"You can't laugh that off. Crane's the best man in the business—absolute tops in the laboratory and practically unbeatable on the witness stand. If they say there's no evidence, Eddie, there's no evidence."

"That's it, chum. No evidence—no murder. No murder—no little fun and games for Connor."

"Righto. Sorry you've been bothered—"

"Come, come, old chap! It's quite all right! A stiff upper lip and all that. Call me any time. It's been *such* fun—"

5

The early afternoon papers missed the autopsy report but carried a lot of sensational material of the SWEATBOX DEATH TRAP FOR JOCKEY variety. Johnny had been popular with the sports writers, and there were several by-line pieces with emotional leads—*The weight gets them all in racing—horses and riders alike. Last night it got little Johnny Mallo. . . .* That sort of thing.

I stuffed the newspapers into the wastebasket—and promptly hauled them out again for piling neatly in the kitchen. Cat owners seldom throw away newspapers.

I wandered around the apartment saying "that's that" to myself and not believing it. Sauki-no-no was still looking out the window, but her new friend was nowhere in sight. A man in gray trousers and a hot-looking blue jacket leaned against the restaurant wall.

The more I tried to crowd the Mallo matter out of my head, the more I kept thinking of one small metal object—a neat chrome light switch that had been clicking on and off in my mind ever since I'd first seen it on the inside wall of Johnny's cabinet.

One movement of one finger would have turned off that deadly battery of hot bulbs—one desperate, fainting gesture toward its familiar location. Yet it had remained, untouched, six inches from his dead hand. It didn't make sense. A man doesn't take nine years of rigid weight control to learn that he can feel faint in a sweat bath.

A picture of me rendering that sort of testimony against Storky Crane's solid facts brought me back to earth. I made a long, cool Forester and water and sat down to sulk in comfort.

Sometime around six the phone rang. Lorry Mallo wondered timidly if—well—if I wasn't too busy—

"I'm terribly worried about—what you said to Mickey."

"Concerning insurance, Lorry?"

"I hope you don't think I'm—heartless, but there seems to be a hurry about it. Dr. Pack told me the insurance company had someone at the—examination."

"I know. Would you like to go to some quiet place for dinner?"

"If you think it would be all right. Any place but here would be such a relief."

"I'll pick you up in half an hour. O.K.?"

"It would be wonderful, Doc. Thank you."

I called Mike Picoletto and asked him to hold the corner booth. He didn't add to my happiness by remarking that it would be dee-lightful to see Mees Storm again. When I told him it wouldn't be Mees Storm tonight, he tsk-ed me.

I killed the half hour contemplating my sins and wondering how much interest Pack had in Lorry's insurance. He'd been prompt enough to report that the company's representative had attended the autopsy. On the other hand, maybe he'd called to tell Lorry they'd gotten away with a very fancy husband purge.

When I rang Lorry from the lobby, she was waiting inside. Very tidy, too, apparently having done her emergency shopping. The little widow was at half-mast. The red, white, and blue set against black may have been mourning, but there was a lot of hope for the future in it.

Picoletto's wasn't crowded, and Mike had staked out the rear corner for us. I got Lorry settled and offered her a cigarette.

"I have my own, thank you, Doc—hope you won't mind." She produced one of those off brands smoked by people who always have to do everything the hard way. I picked up a paper of matches but she made a quick gesture of thanks and had her lighter going in the same movement. Somebody had been very attentive to the young lady.

The waiter took our order and went away. Mike concocts a veal-in-wine arrangement that has kept his dingy place out of bankruptcy for years. He watched us until he was sure I wouldn't order cocktails, then sent over a bottle of chianti—Tuscan and dry. If Katie had been along, he would have brought it himself, beaming and booming Latin extravagancies.

Lorry was subdued and thoughtful. "It doesn't seem very nice to talk about unpleasant things through such a lovely dinner."

"Better than letting them spoil the meal—from the inside." I saw she wasn't going to waste any time mooning over her grief. "There's a lot to talk about."

"There seems to be." She studied the ash tray as she stubbed out her cigarette. "Johnny left nothing but his insurance, Doc—nothing. Can you blame me for being concerned?"

"Of course not. It does seem a little improvident."

"Not improvident. Just, perhaps—ill-advised. My husband decided, years ago, that he'd put everything into insurance. He called it his estate. When we were married, he made his policies over to me. We felt very—secure."

"May I ask how much is concerned?"

"Something more than seventy-five thousand dollars." She said the words without emphasis, as though she'd become very familiar with them.

"The double-indemnity clause makes that a lot of money." A lot of dough, certainly, I thought, to be riding on a vague possibility. "Had Johnny ever discussed what would happen to his insurance if he had a racing accident?"

"He laughed it off—said the track would give me a benefit." She glanced at me under her lashes and looked back at her plate. "You know how it is with race riders."

"Sure. It can't happen to me." The waiter put the food before us. "I don't suppose either of you ever had a thought about—this sort of a possibility?"

"Nobody did—the insurance company or anybody else. It hardly seems fair to save the money for all those premiums and then find you'll end up with a benefit." She gave her food a dismal look. "What can I do, Doc?"

"I don't know." I wondered why the apparently devoted Pack had insisted that Mallo's heart was sound. He either wasn't interested in the insurance or he was interested as hell in covering up the fact that Johnny had been murdered. Maybe it was both. A redhead with a considerable fortune might be harder to get. I said, "Did Ralph Pack tell you the results of the autopsy?"

"Yes. He said there wasn't the slightest possibility that my husband had been—injured before he went into the cabinet. Not enough to cause his death."

"That's right. The facts seem to point that out. Have you got some other idea, Lorry?"

"No. Mickey suggested that you had." She hesitated. "Have you?"

"I did have, before the police report came in. Johnny had been asking for trouble."

"How?" She seemed surprised. "I know he had a row with Mickey, but surely that wouldn't have been too serious. They were always scrapping."

"Do you know anything about the Nautilus deal?"

"The Nautilus deal?" No guile. "Nautilus is a running horse. I don't know anything about a deal."

"All right. Forget it. The deal never came off. What about Johnny's relations with Huck Trask? How did they get along?"

"They hated each other. I don't think they've exchanged a civil word for several years now."

"Do you know why?"

Lorry laughed without smiling. "Trask and his wife made a fool of Johnny four years ago in Florida."

"Will you tell me about it?"

"Can I take off this damned hat?"

"You can throw it away for my dough."

She smiled, brightened up. "What's the matter with it? Doesn't it do anything for me?"

"Sure it does. It makes people want you to take it off." Time out, apparently, for the light touch. She tossed the hat on an extra chair and patted her blazing hair.

"Better?"

"Much. Now tell me about Florida."

"Well, it was just one of those things that happen when people are—oh—sort of at loose ends like you get in Miami during the season. Johnny was top rider down there that winter and was not only making a lot of money, but was getting terrific publicity."

"I remember. He rode Pitterpat in The Widener."

"That's right. I was operating the switchboard in his hotel and he was running around with Eve. She was singing in a club—I forgot which one, but it wasn't too swanky."

"Was Trask around at the time?"

"Yes. We were all—sort of friends. Huck was in a funny spot because he was crazy about Eve and at the same time, wanted to handle Johnny's riding engagements. He had a couple of other riders and was trying to make a go of it."

"How about Mickey? Where was he?"

"Mick was just a kid, then, of course, but he had his working papers and was galloping horses for Frank Latch. He used to come around the switchboard and make cracks about Johnny's big blonde. He knew it burned me up—"

"Why? Were you fond of Johnny at that time?"

Lorry grinned slyly. "Very. He used to take me out and talk about Eve—how she ought to be in the big time."

"Oh? That way, eh?"

"Not for long. One night, toward the end of the season, there was a grand three-way bust-up. Johnny never would talk much about it. Eve had been up in his suite and I think he threw her out. She came raging down to the lobby, made a couple of nasty cracks at me, and stalked out. Half an hour later Huck Trask came in and went up to the suite. I was afraid they'd fight but Huck came down again in a few minutes looking very pleased with himself."

"But Trask never did get Johnny's book."

"No. My husband refused to change agents."

"What do you think the row was about?"

"I've thought of a lot of things. The one that makes most sense is that Huck and Eve were about to be—or actually were— married at the time."

"The old Army game. Could have been, at that—and very embarrassing for Johnny." He wouldn't have talked too much about that around home. "So when Mickey started hanging around with the Trasks, here in New York, Johnny was really burned."

The girl fished around under the table with her foot—probably looking for a stray shoe. "He disliked it so much, that I think he's been trying to get something on Huck ever since."

"And you think he might have found something?"

"I don't know; There was plenty of reason for me to believe that the Trasks were under some sort of pressure." Lorry looked directly at me for a moment, then said, "Hell, Doc; I might as well tell you the rest of it."

She reached over to the next chair and fished around in her pocketbook. Finally she came up with a telegram and handed it to me. It read

TERRIBLY IMPORTANT SEE YOU AT ONCE STOP FREE EIGHT TONIGHT HOME STOP OTHERS GOING TO OFFICE SO HAVE OP-PORTUNITY TO DISCUSS MOST URGENT BUSINESS

CORKY

"Who's Corky?"

"Eve Corcoran Trask. I found the wire in Johnny's bathrobe pocket before I called the doctor. He'd probably intended to destroy it."

"Do you know whether he kept the date?" The message had been delivered on Friday afternoon, care of the secretary's office at the track.

"I—think he did. He said he had to go some place."

"Have you made any guesses as to what it could have been about?" There didn't seem to be any nicer way to put it.

She raised her head slowly, looked me straight in the eyes, and said, "No."

There wasn't too much to say after that, and we finished dinner on small talk and race-track reminiscences. Lorry Mallo was under a tremendous strain and was taking it damned well. As we left, she carried her hat in her hand and walked with a straight back.

As we got to the door, Mike called me aside with many apologies. "Look, Doc; you got trouble or somepin'?"

"No trouble, Mike. The woman I'm with is just a good friend. Katie is out in—"

"No. No, Doc. I do not mean the woman. I mean trouble like with the cops. They lookin' for you or maybe the lady?"

"The cops? No. Why?"

"They's a guy outside followed you when you come in. I seen him tail you here in a cab. Just now I seen him again—standin' across the side street. I sneaked in the keetchin an' looked. He's got a cab waitin' halfway down the block. You better look out, eh?"

"It's all right, Mike." I knew it wasn't any of Eddie's men, and I didn't feel too good about it. "Tell me. Was he a little man—like a jockey?"

"Not like a jockey. Pretty good-size guy—maybe almos' so beeg as you. He's got gray pants an' a blue coat. You better be careful, my fran', sometimes you get inna lotta trouble." He shook hands as if I were leaving to face a firing squad.

"Thanks, Mike. I'll watch my step." The gray pants and blue coat sounded hazily familiar, but I didn't get them placed. I tabbed the man for Trask and wondered what he would be looking for. I couldn't quite see Pack skulking the alleys, but a jealous man is a jealous man any place you find him.

We flagged a cab and took off. I didn't see the tail's cab, either then or as I delivered Lorry at her door.

She thanked me sweetly, and I promised to try to get her something better than a benefit in the way of a future, thereby planting myself in the middle of the damned thing again.

I walked home, turning in on Broadway at Fifty-first, and headed south. As I approached Forty-eighth and started to cross, I saw a man standing in the shadow of one of our allegedly decorative columns. He was watching the street alertly.

He wore gray slacks and a hot-looking blue jacket.

6

I beat it back to the sidewalk and walked behind people almost to Forty-seventh, then cut across Broadway and went in
through the service entrance. The janitor wasn't around, so I
took the rear stairway that leads to the lobby, and landed in the
entry not ten feet away from the guy.

The stone column would provide as good a hiding place for
me, on one side, as it had for him on the other. I edged to the
doorway and peeked around. He must have been certain I hadn't
entered the building, having followed me away from the restaurant. He'd probably tailed my empty cab away. As I caught a
glimpse of him, he had his back turned.

I reached out and grabbed him by the collar, dragged him
back through the doorway before he could organize himself. He
made comic-strip noises and went for a gun, which is not for
the funny papers. I gave him another yank and swung a short
right, in and up. He took it on the jaw and started down, still
clawing for the shoulder holster. I swung hard with my left, felt
it register, and grabbed for the gun with both hands. He fell,
and I came up with a blue thirty-eight.

The man never got any farther than his hands and knees.
He crawled around awhile, shaking his head and paying a lot of
attention to the floor. Then he wiped the back of his hand
across his mouth, and turned his head sideways, trying to see me.

"Hello, Doc."

"Get up."

He got slowly to his feet. I held the gun away and grabbed him with my left hand, but he showed no interest in me whatever; kept trying to get a hand to his mouth. When I eased off on him a little, he reached in and hauled out a very complicated-looking arrangement of steel and metal, on which teeth were strung at casual intervals. He studied it carefully, put it back, and chomped on it a couple of times. Then he looked up, and I recognized him.

"Bust it, Elegant?"

"Don't feel like it. The damn thing set me back a hundred and ninety bucks." He dug up a handkerchief and started to wipe his face. "Maybe someday I'll learn better than to take these two-bit jobs. You can't win."

"Let's go upstairs. You can tell me about it while you wash up."

He gave me a questioning look. "I got nothing to tell you, Doc."

"Upstairs, Elegant. Maybe I'll buy you a drink." I steered him to the elevator, opened the gate, and shoved him in. It wouldn't have done him any good to run, because I knew where to find him. Elegant Johnson was a third-rate private detective, and I could look him up in the phone book.

I fixed him a drink while he dabbed his face in the washbowl. He didn't look too elegant when he came out—a lean, tired-looking guy with deep-set blue eyes and black hair. Nobody knows where he got his name. That sort of thing happens around our end of town. Probably some long-forgotten incident.

He sat in the big chair and accepted the whisky gratefully. I gave him a minute before I went to work on him.

"O.K., Elegant, let's hear about it. You were watching the apartment earlier today and followed me to Mike Picoletto's. Why?"

He took a big drink, leaned back, and sighed. "Nothing much to it, Doc. Just what you'd expect. A client hires me to tail you and report your activities—strictly a routine surveillance job. Somebody trying to divorce you?"

"Not yet. Who's the client?"

"Hell! You know better than to ask that."

"I'm damned well going to find out, one way or another."

"I might as well take my bridge out this time. You wouldn't believe me anyway." He gave me a punchy grin.

"Why not?"

"Because I don't know who my client is." Johnson spread his hands and shrugged his shoulders. "I couldn't tell you if I wanted to. We get a lot of jobs like that."

I didn't believe him, of course. "You know what you're mixed up in, Elegant?"

"No." He drank some of the whisky out of the good side of his mouth. "Whatever it is, it won't be the first time."

"Probably not. It's a homicide—Grade A. You're up to your neck in it."

"A homicide?" He was concerned by that time. "Something you're working on with Marsh?"

"The cops aren't on it actively yet, but they will be when they learn some things I know. Also some things you know, Johnson." Then I snapped it at him. "Let's have it. Who's your client?"

He shook his head slowly. "You can only get just so tough with me, Doc, then you have to start slapping me around. A lot of people have tried to do that. You've got my gun on you, but you won't shoot anybody. Don't try to kid me."

I felt like a frustrated adolescent. "Of course I won't shoot anybody! What I'm trying to tell you is that this isn't any routine two-bit job as you call it. You're working for a killer, you damned fool. What do you suppose will happen to your license?"

Elegant ruffled up his thin hair. "All right, Doc. So I been working for a killer. Now I'm off the case. So I tell you again, I don't know who the guy is I been working for. I got the job from Sam Fenner, the lawyer, this morning."

Sam Fenner had been at the autopsy! "I don't know him."

"Sam does a lot of work for the horse people—trainers and jockeys and like that."

"What jockeys? Johnny Mallo, maybe?"

"I don't know who. He defended the driver in the vanning accident last year when that good horse was killed—Rig—Rig something."

"Rigaloft." The negligent truckman had gotten off lightly. "Maybe I'll buy that, Elegant." I gave him back his gun, and he shoved it into the clip. "Now get off my tail—and stay off!"

"I wouldn't touch you with a ten-foot pole." He boosted himself out of the chair. "Look, Doc, I got a card in my pocket that says I can make a living peeking. I do all right at it most of the time. I want to keep that ticket, and horsing around in a homicide for somebody I don't know is a good way to lose it. You won't see me any more—professionally. Of course if you should invite me up for a drink—" He looked steadily at my right hand. "You crack a knuckle, Doc?"

I closed my fist, and it hurt like hell. It looked a little swollen. "Hey! Maybe I did!"

He gave me a beat-up grin. "Well, how do you like that?" Said it like Mel Allen. "I got no glass jaw, eh, champ? I go to m' hands and knees, but I stay off the deck! Right?"

"Right, Elegant. You take a nice punch."

"I sure as hell am in the right business for it." He put on his hat and headed for the door. "Well, see you around, Doc."

"Yes. Do that, shamus—keep your bridge in."

I listened him down in the elevator, and wondered which of the Mallo-Trask-Pack contingent I'd frightened badly enough to put a professional on me. I may have made something of a gag of my encounter with Elegant Johnson, but I took him plenty seriously.

I was in a position which pretty well guaranteed my continued interest in the affair whether I liked it or not. The news of the autopsy would inform one and all that the police had no further interest in Mallo's death. That left me as the only threat to the killer's safety—if there was a killer, which seemed likely enough. If I didn't push him too hard he'd simply try to bully me off the case. If I happened to come up with some of the answers—who knows? If it were certain of the people concerned, it might turn out to be very tough.

I couldn't have lost any sleep over it. I woke up next morning with the sound of church bells in my ears and the soft pad of Sauki-no-no's feet as she paced up and down my back. When she recognized signs of life she rasped out some throaty remarks which I took to be a request for food.

"What's the matter, Mom? Want your breakfast?"

She jumped off the bed and beat it for the kitchen, where she rattled papers vigorously. By the time I was up she was standing in the doorway waiting for me. I wouldn't have batted an eye if she had asked me for a toothbrush.

I'd just finished thawing the meat when Eddie Marsh started battering down my door—a habit which is probably a holdover from the harness days when he demanded entry to places of even less repute. When I let him in, he had an armload of packages. It would be a celebratory breakfast—a sign that his bachelor quarters had got too small for him or that he had something on his mind.

"What you got, copper?"

"The works! Kidneys, eggs, live orange juice, and non-canned cream." We unloaded the stuff in the kitchen, and Eddie put a dish towel around his waist. "How's your no-murder case coming?"

"Curious already?"

"A gentle rib, chum. The only kind of homicide I get curious about is one where somebody kills somebody." He started unwrapping the kidneys. "That kind you just ain't got."

"I wouldn't bet on it if I were you." It was a casual crack, but it stopped him short. He stood with a half-wound string in his hands.

"You got something, Doc?"

"I've got at least four people with motives. Are you satisfied that the guy wasn't murdered?"

"The department's gold-plated experts say so."

"They didn't say anything of the sort. That's why they're experts. They said that they *found* no evidence of murder. No scientific man would say there *wasn't* any—even if that were his opinion."

"That's a lot of bones and no meat, kid." Eddie took yesterday's burned toast out of the oven and turned on the broiler. "Maybe you can tell me how Mallo could have been murdered."

"*Could* have been? Sure I can."

He looked at me searchingly for an instant and went on splitting kidneys. Only sissies soak them. "It'll be dull, but get on with it."

"He could have been electrocuted."

"Rats! You really reached for that one! We're not stupid, you know. We went into that thoroughly—no burn, no short circuit, no fuse blown. First thing we thought of."

"If you'd been with Johnny Mallo Friday afternoon and talked to the other people with me, the first thing you'd thought of would be murder." I was having fun, but I got a growing conviction that I was making sense too. "Then you would have gone into that switch to see if it had been tampered with—then repaired."

He paused with his hand under the broiler, yanked it out, and stared at me. "Damn you, Doc, if you've been holding out on me again—"

"I haven't. The room's still sealed. Incidentally, I'd like to get in there for another look."

"Help yourself. I called Mrs. Mallo this morning, so it's probably open already." He finished putting the kidneys in and closed the oven door; got out a frying pan and frowned at it. "Damn!"

"What's the matter? Pan dirty?"

"No. You're annoying as hell."

"Provocative, what? I got another hypothesis."

"All right."

"Mallo stays thirty-five minutes in the box, starts to climb out, pooped, and a guy wrestles him back in. He'd handle easily and pass out quickly—thermotaxic load. Neat?"

"Mrs. Mallo would have to be a party to it."

"Can you think of a nicer party?"

"Good triangle."

"The thing's got more triangles than Euclid. Figure it out— with the dead one stretched out from A to B. Put Mickey and

Trask on the sides—a kind of slaunchwise arrangement, but it'll do. Maybe Johnny got them into trouble, and one of them killed him by switch-fixing."

"How about the Mallo woman? She'd have to know about it."

"Maybe not. We don't know, yet, when she was away from the apartment Friday—and for how long." Actually, we had only her statement that she'd been in the apartment during the evening. "But let's set up another triangle. Use Pack and Lorry for the sides."

Eddie said, "I like that one."

"It's worth thinking about. The guy's apparently gone on the little widow and—with a nice, scientifically planned killing—he fits pretty well."

"How about the two babes? That would be decorative."

"And effective. There's a lot of boiler pressure in the pair of them—also another angle I learned last night." I told him about Eve's wire. "The Trask woman would definitely be the kind to fight her way out of a hole—her husband would, too, for that matter."

"Let's make it the croaker, Doc." Eddie broke eggs into a bowl, using one hand, like a soda jerker. "We haven't had a sawbones down there in years. But he wouldn't have called you if he'd killed Mallo."

"I think he would have. He even acted a little that way. He just stalked around and said, in effect, of course, 'I am about to certify that this gent died from dehydration caused by fainting in a sweat bath. I simply called you in as a witness to my findings. That'll be all, thank you, Doctor.'"

Eddie nodded. "Sure. He might as well have said, 'I have just knocked this joker off because I'm in love with his wife. The fact that he may not get any insurance makes me look good. You make me look better, Doctor, because neither you nor anybody else will ever know how I did it.'"

"Exactly. And from here it looks like he might get away with it."

"Wouldn't it be peachy if it turned out to be something exotic like curare and a blowpipe!" Marsh dumped the eggs into the pan. "Set the table and we'll eat."

The food was too good for serious talk, so we spent most of the time eating. A couple of cigarettes after breakfast Eddie leaned his chair against the wall and grinned contentedly at me.

"Look here, Brain Trust; your hypotheses make dandy chatter, but I'm afraid they won't catch you any killers. Me, I'm a factual guy—trained that way by the best police department in the world. We can take the damnedest mess of ill-assorted stuff you ever saw and make a tight, integrated case out of it. But the stuff is factual, Doc—not conjectural."

"Sure! I know all that, but—"

"Wait a minute. You're something else again. You don't know a fact from your elbow, but you've got a hell of a talent for understanding the relations between facts."

"That's white of you, pal."

"Don't get defensive. We've wound up some pretty sensational cases together, and I've learned not to sell you short." He bounced his chair down and began to pile up dishes. "This time you've got a fine fence and no posts.

Go get yourself a couple of facts so I can reopen the thing if there's enough to work on. Make sense?"

It did. There didn't seem to be any reason to mention Elegant Johnson, or to expose Mickey to minor charges. The problem would be to find out *why* Elegant Johnson and *who* was hurt by young Mallo's deal. They could easily be pieces of the same fact. Eddie piled plates in the sink and took his coat off. "How about washing some dishes?"

"Did I ever fail you in a time of need?"

"Oh, brother! Remember the time in Boston—?"

"Let's get at it."

As we slopped through the chores I kept wondering where I'd get any facts. They wouldn't come as physical findings—at least it seemed improbable after Storky Crane's report.

They would come as words forced out of people because they didn't dare hold them any longer—driven out of them for self-preservation, like animals are driven before a forest fire.

The thing to do, of course, was start a fire.

7

In the matter of starting a fire, the most likely piece of tinder at hand seemed to me the wire Eve had sent to Johnny at the track—the *Corky* telegram. If I could drop a carefully shielded spark into that, I might start myself quite a blaze.

Any time a woman as smart as la Trask sends her ex-sweetheart a message that the old man's out, come and see me, there's inflammable material around somewhere. Maybe it wouldn't be just a match-dropping job, but there were a lot of things lying around to rub together.

Lorry Mallo cheerfully gave me the Trask home address, adding some caustic remarks about whether I prized my virtue. If my guess was any good, Huck would be down at his one-way office sorting out horses for Monday, and his helpmeet would be lolling out her Sunday afternoon at home.

Shortly after two I cabbed over. It was an oldish apartment building, and I sent up my name from the lobby.

The gent on the desk gave me the taxidermist's eye and admitted that Mrs. Trask was in and would see me. It was painful for him—seemed like little Eva didn't rate too high on his calling list. As I went up, I wondered if something had gone on recently to disturb the management, or whether the guy had been trying to exchange witticisms with the lady.

When she opened the door I played it straight. "Hello! Huck in?"

In a secretive stage whisper she said, "No. Come in." Disguised as some sort of tremendously healthy butterfly in yards of lavender robe—complete with long, droopy wings—she swooped down on me, grabbed my hat, clutched my arm with the other hand, and kicked the door closed with a large muled foot.

"There's drinking going on in here, Doctor. I hope you won't be offended."

"Some of my best friends drink. What you got?"

She hauled me off into a good-sized, overstuffed living room and dropped me into a chair. "A pitcher of Jack Roses, my little pal, and not too much grenadine. How does that strike you?"

"Well, I'll tell you." I gave it the Bill Fields. "In the past, I have been stricken mightily by such a concoction. On the other hand, a little of the Pink Panther of a Sunday afternoon . . ."

"You're in! Hold your cup." I didn't see any receptacle thereabouts except a heavy glass affair that looked like a vase. "Right there beside you. Say when!"

"This thing?"

"What do you want? A test tube?" I shoved it out and she poured, talking steadily. "Look, Doc! Every glass, no matter how big it is, has a bottom and a top—"

"Hey! Hold it!" She poured for a few more words and let up.

"—a bottom and a top. It's a fella's own responsibility how far he wants his liquor from either one." She hoisted her goblet. "Here's how!"

We drank, chatted, and drank some more. In the absence of good bourbon whisky, well-seasoned apple brandy can be a cup of considerable cheer, even when gilded with lemon juice and grenadine. After a while Eve put her drink down and said, "Now what'll we play?"

"I'm playing detective—still trying to make some sense out of Johnny Mallo's death."

She looked at me steadily for a moment. "Why you, Doc?"

"Oh, several reasons, I guess. Johnny invited me in, of course, in the first place. Now somebody's trying to invite me out. I'm kind of perverse when people start shoving me around."

"Who's inviting you out?"

"You know Sam Fenner?"

"Sure I know him. He's a shyster lawyer. Is Sam pushing you around?"

"By indirection. Somebody hired him to have me—watched."

"I see." She fooled with her purple wings, laying them out carefully beside her and smoothing them. "Look, Doc, what doesn't make sense about Johnny's death?"

Her perfectly natural question alerted me. "Too much co-incidence. Too many people wanted him out of the picture just when he—was taken out."

"What people, for instance?"

"Maybe some people who didn't want the Nautilus fix to come to light."

Eve got up and walked—thoughtfully, it seemed to me—across the room to bring back a silver box. She sat down and flipped the lid open.

"Cigarette, Doc?"

"Thanks." I helped the act by fussing with the lighter.

"Huck told you, didn't he, that he was going to handle Mickey's book?"

"He said he wanted to—"

"Do you think he'd start out by getting the boy set down for life?"

"Probably not—if he knew that Mickey was going to leave betting slips around." I didn't figure it would do much good to ask her if Trask needed money. "Can you be as convincing about what your husband would do if he thought Johnny might put him out of business?"

She smiled very pleasantly. "No. Let's have a drink."

We had a drink. I was getting no place except a little tight. Time, now, to drop a few lighted matches around. "I'd like to know where Johnny Mallo was on Friday evening."

Whatever effect it had on her, I had to read off the bottom of the glass. When she put it down she said, "What good would that do?"

"I've got a hunch that Johnny had some sort of a deal on, and that some phase of that deal precipitated the rest." I waited for her to offer something, then went on. "I thought you might know about it."

She filled up the glasses again. Her aim was a little off, but otherwise she seemed sober enough. But she wasn't saying anything. I caught a feeling of stubborn resistance in her. I thought I'd try to soften it up.

"Eve, Johnny was a good kid. He didn't deserve a break like that."

The woman gave me a long, straight look. "That's a matter of opinion, Doc."

That could be the bust-up in Florida. I let it go. "I hoped you could help me locate him as of, say, eight to ten Friday night."

"Have you asked his wife?"

"She says he had an engagement somewhere."

"He didn't tell her where he was going?"

"No. Nor *why*, Eve." I made it as significant as I could. It must have been hammy. She laughed.

"You talk like my mother."

"What do you mean?"

"Skip it! Whyn't' you drink your drink?"

Anything to please! I picked up my vase. "Why not? I'm not driving."

"The hell you're not!"

"Driving?"

"That's right. Driving me. What's more, Doccy, you better give it up or Mama will take this nice, nourishing pitcher and lock herself in the bedroom with it."

I gulped down some of the stuff. "It's too bad you can't see your way clear to help. I'm certain there'll be a thorough investigation before long."

"I understood the police had dropped it."

"The insurance people won't drop it—so long as Lorry presses her claim."

"Oh?"

"Sure. That way, the whole thing's in reverse. The insurance investigators will go running around saying little prayers they don't find a killer or a cause of accident, and Lorry stands to win a hell of a lot of dough if she can find one."

I stood up and went across the room for my hat. There were big wrinkles in the floor and it was a rough crossing, but I managed it with some dignity. Eve said, "Where you going?"

"I'm going downstairs and get hold of the management or the doorman or somebody. I want to find out what time Johnny left here Friday night." I leaned nonchalantly against the good, steady doorframe. "Your telegram was in Mallo's bathrobe' pocket. He didn't have a chance to get rid of it. He didn't have a chance—period."

The big purple butterfly drooped. She stared into her cocktail and her head swayed from side to side. "So long, Eve. I'll see you around. Thanks for the drink."

She looked up and gave me a tired grin. "The *drinks*, Doc."

"Sorry. Thanks for the drinks."

"Are you bullying me, or are you really leaving?"

"I intended to bully you as far as the door. Then, if you didn't change your mind, I was leaving."

Eve brushed her hair back with her forearm like she'd had her hands in flour. "Oh, Doc, there's so much to it, goddamit; so much from a long time back. Stuff that should have stayed back there and wouldn't!" She looked around as if she were trying to find some place to get out. "I can't help anybody without hurting everybody."

"Like who?"

"Huck. Mickey. Myself." She frowned at her drink. "Even Johnny."

"How much does Lorry know?"

I thought my forest fire was in full blaze for a moment. The big butterfly was suddenly transformed into a hawk, then it was over. She untied her fingers and smiled. "Lorry Mallo knows a great deal, Doc. She knows how to take hold of a man and squeeze him until his principles run out of him like blood—until he's bled white of every decent idea he ever had."

"Do you care to explain that?"

"No, my friend, I do not care to explain that." She picked up her glass. "We will now drink."

"Look, Eve; right now I'm not too much concerned about your having seen Johnny on Friday night. I have a hunch that would be an involvement—a complication—rather than the sort of direct thing I need at the moment. I think I want to know if Johnny saw a man on Friday night."

She turned to me with a lopsided smile. "I think that's what you want to know too." She nodded her head sagely. "A very smart man."

Pay dirt! "Yes. He would have to be smart. He would have to know a good deal about"—I didn't want to mention electricity—"science. Maybe he should be strong too."

"What would you say if I should name this musc'lar man of science for you?" She leaned toward me. "If I should tell you that science is his *racket?*"

"I'd say thank you very much, then go way and leave you alone to enjoy the rest of your drinks in peace." It had to be Pack, of course, and I was disappointed. Eve would probably retail some of the gossip that had, apparently, been going around their little clan. "Did Johnny see such a man that night?"

"It is my earnest opinion that he did. It was also Johnny's earnest opinion that he was going to." She straightened her shoulders, frowned. "Doc, if you want to know where Johnny was on Friday night, go and ask the Mallo family physician."

"What time did Johnny see Pack? Right after he left here?"

I watched her think it over. She looked fixedly at several objects around the room—a focusing process not unknown to those who are given to ingesting large quantities of such things as applejack. When she'd made it around to me, she looked remarkably sober.

"You're a mean little man, aren't you!"

"Am I?"

"Yes." She shook her head—a mistake. Squeezed her eyes shut and opened them again. "Yes. I'm afraid you're a mean little man." She shook her finger this time, then gave me a benedictory smile. "But you're a pretty little man, so I'm going to tell you something."

"What?"

"Yes." Eve stood up carefully and came over to me.

"Yes, what?"

"Yes . . . right after he left here. He came at quarter past eight and sat . . ." Long pause. "You know what, Doc? If he was here now, he'd be sitting on our beau'ful pitcher!"

"What time did he leave?"

"He left at quarter to nine pree-cisely—pree-cisely! And that, my frien', among persons of culture, means *no kidding.*"

"Did he have an appointment with Pack?"

"He just said, 'I gotta see Ralph,' and left."

You can't shoot a guy for trying, so I said, "Eve, would it do me any good to know why you had to see Johnny—why you wired him?"

She turned away from me, brushed her hair back with her forearm again. "No—no, it wouldn't do anybody any good"— she took a couple of steps forward—"now."

As she lurched I went to her, put my hand on her arm. She shook it off, took dead aim on the pitcher, and set sail. Her shoulders kept trying to slump and she kept pulling them back. She got the pitcher by the handle. It hung slaunchways at the end of a limp arm. She said, "There's nothing more I can do to help—anybody."

Then she lugged the pitcher through the bedroom door and there was a sound as she put it down on something. The mules hit the floor—one—two. I heard her sob and went in. I sat down on the bed and took her hand. "Forget it, Eve. I'm not the cops, you know. Maybe you can't help anybody, the way things are. Maybe it's time for somebody to help you."

She pressed my hand and presented a teary grin. "Thanks, Doc. You're a good guy, and I'm goin' to give you some advice."

"I need it, Lord knows. What?"

"Put up your lance, Doc. It's strictly a windmill." She laughed and reached over for the pitcher. "Now you'd better get the hell out of here. Old Santa Claus will be coming home any minute."

I went back to the living room and, for some reason which I have since been unable to explain, finished the half pint of Jack Roses which I'd left in my vase.

I groped my way down to the building entrance and debouched—debauched.

8

When I got back to the apartment, I was greeted by bitter complaints from Sauki-no-no. She squatted in the middle of the living-room rug and glared at me. I'd never seen her in that crouching pose and wondered if something could be wrong.

"What's the matter, old lady? You got trouble?"

Then I saw her coming—flying toward my face with forelegs wide and eyes blazing. Applejack glued me to the spot. I threw out my arms too late and she flashed between them. Next thing I knew, she was on my shoulder, rubbing her whiskers against my chin and purring like an outboard.

I pretended I hadn't been scared and petted her awhile. After what seemed a courteous interval, I leaned over the couch and she jumped off, very well pleased about the whole thing. I was pretty well pleased myself. Apparently the damned cat liked me.

Just to show you how life is, however, I remembered I hadn't given her her cod-liver oil and had to do it right then—a troublesome process for both of us.

While I was doing the chores I got to thinking about Ralph Pack. For one reason or another Eve Trask might be taking a lot of things for granted. Her feelings about Lorry Mallo could well have created a nasty situation in her mind—whether with Pack or anyone else.

The obscure method—circumstances—of Mallo's death seemed to point out the physician as a likely prospect. Whoever killed Johnny was either thoroughly well informed—or a complete fool. After all, when you murder someone, you want to be reasonably sure he doesn't recover and chide you for it. You could ask a dozen registered nurses, even physicians, how long it would take to kill a man by dehydration, and you'd get a dozen different answers.

For that matter, it's about as hard to guess how long, and at what temperatures, it takes to kill a man's conscience with redheads. Pack would know about the insurance problem if he'd given it any thought at all, but maybe the money didn't count. Certainly making the death look like a reducing accident would remove at least one powerful motive.

I took a prolonged cold shower—a process which I dislike intensely but which hair-shirted me into reasonable sobriety. Then I called Pack.

When I announced myself, he gave me a raised eyebrow. "Oh?" Then, "Good evening, Dr. Connor." Smug as hell.

"I understand you attended the Mallo autopsy."

"I did." There were minor room sounds back of his voice. "Were you informed of the findings?"

"Yes. Rather completely."

"Now, perhaps"—he shifted from smug to unctuous—"you'll understand the position I took over your calling the police on Friday night—Saturday morning."

"I think I do." I said it without implication, but he wouldn't have it that way. I heard the clinking of glassware in the distant background.

"What do you mean 'you think you do,' Doctor? I fail to understand how, as an amateur detective, you could have any further interest in the matter. Mallo's death was plainly—"

"I'd like to talk with you as soon as possible."

"What about, if I may ask?"

He was up on about seventeen hands of high horse, and I figured it was time for me to cut him down to my size. I didn't care for the amateur-detective crack. I read the next line but this time, with implications. "I want to talk to you about Lorry Mallo, Pack."

He didn't sputter, but it would have been better for his nervous system if he had. "Mrs. Mallo? Look here, Connor, it seems to me that you are taking—"

"Mrs. Mallo has consulted me about some of the medico-legal aspects of her husband's insurance. I am undertaking to help her with them—largely to see that she's not left in reduced circumstances. The least you can do is to give me a little co-operation. You *are* fond of Lorry, aren't you?"

He started out stuffy as hell. *"Fond* of her? My dear Dr. Connor; John Mallo has been my patient for more than—"

He began to think better of it when I said: "I thought you were a good friend of the Mallos."

"Of course I've been a good friend of theirs; something of a counselor to the young people as well as Mallo's physician almost since their marriage. If you put it that way . . ."

I gave him an out and he came up halter-broken. "Perhaps I stated myself awkwardly, Doctor?"

"Naturally—in the light of our pleasant association—I'm fond of Mrs. Mallo." It practically dripped. "How can I be of service?"

"I'd like to come over and talk with you."

"Splendid. I shall be free within the hour."

A woman's voice in the background said, "Don't let him come here—"

The room sounds stopped suddenly with a dull plop that suggested a hand on the transmitter. I didn't give Pack a chance to change his mind; said, "Thanks. I'll see you then." Hung up.

The voice had been Lorry Mallo's.

While I dressed I did some mental prowling on the subject of Ralph Pack and Johnny's redheaded widow. One of Eddie's and my triangles, with the dead man lying horizontally from A to B. Lorry and the young physician looked as well up there with their heads together at C as any of the others.

I got hungry and opened a can of chile, consumed it along with some pieces of rat cheese I found drying out in the refrigerator. One of the more obscure reasons Katie uses for not marrying me is that I couldn't adapt myself to civilized meals, and would eat exclusively from refrigerator leftovers. She claims that proper leftovers are hard to plan and prepare.

I took my time getting across town to Pack's office—a very proper first-floor apartment-house setup that probably

contained living quarters somewhere in the rear. Expensive.
Maybe the insurance money wouldn't mean much to him, at that.

The guy stuck his head out the office door and shoved a
copy of the *Medical Journal* into my hand; said he'd be right
with me. I read a paper on "The Comparative Vestibular Indices
of Pigeons in the Presence of Certain Alkaloids." There was
nothing in it that would help the Post Office Department with
its pigeon problem, or tell me anything about my own wavering
vestibular responses, for that matter. Pack finally threw open
the door and gave me the Roxy steer.

"Come in, Doctor! Sit down. I don't make a habit of Sunday-
evening office hours—er—do you?" He wasn't flustered as he
added, "Oh! Of course! You're not in regular practice."

"Tuesday and Thursday mornings." I sat down. Pack fumbled with some stuff on his desk and eased himself into his big
leather posture chair.

"Very interesting!" He smiled disagreeably. "Any special—
emphasis?"

"In my neighborhood, malnutrition and its collateral dis-
turbances. We also do quite a business in hangovers around the
holidays."

"I see." He was, as I had intended, a little shocked. "Now
tell me, Connor; what, exactly, do you want of me?"

"I'd like to know just when you saw any of the Mallo family
for the first time on Friday night—or Saturday morning?"

"Why would that be of any importance in connection with
young Mallo's insurance?" He plainly didn't like the line of
questioning.

"If you've given any thought to the matter, you'll realize
that, beyond premiums paid in, Mrs. Mallo stands a very good
chance of receiving no benefits whatever if her husband's death
was the direct result of routine reducing. I don't believe it was.
I'm trying to locate all the people concerned, as of Friday night."

Pack took a cigarette, tapped it thoughtfully, then chucked
it aside. "That again! You still think there was something—
criminal, irregular—about Mallo's death?"

"I do—"

"Why do you continue to embarrass Mrs. Mallo when the police have investigated the whole thing and—"

"Look, Pack, I don't want to embarrass Mrs. Mallo. I don't want to embarrass you or the Trasks or Mickey, but I'm damned well going to, if I don't get some simple facts instead of lies and evasions!"

"That's pretty strong talk, Connor." He was quiet, but he felt sandpaper rough for the first time since I'd met him. "You better be able to back it up."

"I'll back it up. In court, if necessary."

"And how have you classed me? Evader or liar?" His lips hardly moved. I found myself in a stare-me-down contest. I lit a cigarette before it got silly.

"Neither yet. I can tell better when you decide to answer my question. When—say between six o'clock on Friday evening and the time you called me Saturday morning—was the first time you saw any of the Mallo family?"

Pack took up the cigarette again and lit it. He leaned back in the big chair, drooped the butt from his lips, and carefully started to play here's-the-church-and-here's-the-steeple. After he'd gone through the process twice, I said, "Why don't you do and-here's-all-the-people? That's the best part."

He looked at me as though I were ready for the chloral hydrate and a wet sheet. "What's that?"

"Nothing. Sorry to interrupt your thinking. You were about to answer my question."

"As a matter of fact, Connor, I was deciding whether to answer your question at all. I can't see what possible bearing it could have on this—unfortunate affair."

"It might have none at all and it might, conceivably, start somebody to the electric chair."

Pack laughed—strictly a sound effect. "Who?"

"Somebody who had some contact with Johnny Mallo Friday evening—somebody who hated him or was afraid of him or was in love with his wife."

The guy stamped to his feet. "Damn you, Connor, that'll be enough out of you! I ought to—"

I made myself stay in my chair. "You ought to sit down and stop trying to implicate yourself. If you didn't see Mallo Friday night, just say so!"

"All right, all *right!* I didn't see Mallo Friday night. The first I saw of any of the Mallos was at approximately three-fifty Saturday morning when I went to the apartment. Does that satisfy you?"

"Perfectly." I got up and went for my hat. "Thank you."

"You're going?"

"Of course." I waited. "You surprised?"

"Quite." He put out his cigarette and smiled at the ash tray. "Is *that* all you wanted of me, Connor?"

"That's all."

"I *am* a rather busy man, you know. I haven't yet limited my practice to hangovers."

I think you'll agree he asked for it—or am I too touchy? Anyway, I burned. "I didn't know whether it would take one question or twenty, Doctor. The first one did it."

"Did what?"

"Got you classified—took you out of the evasive group and put you in with the liars." I said it as quietly as I could under the circumstances. Pack stalked around from behind the desk. I got rid of my hat—put it on. You can't hurt a guy with a hat. He kept coming; stopped with his face a foot from mine.

"Get out!"

We did the strong-man tableau—clash of wills and what not—for a few seconds. Seems juvenile, now, but it could have been tough. When I decided he wasn't going to jump me, I said, "I could be wrong, Pack. Johnny Mallo set out at eight forty-five on Friday night to see you somewhere at nine. It may have been an appointment and it may not. I came here with the impression that he had seen you."

"Never mind the apology. Get out!" He crowded me a little. I moved to the door. Pack didn't follow. I decided to try one more shot in the dark. "What do you know about an attorney by the name of Sam Fenner?"

He batted his eyes; closed the door in my face. I think maybe he himself was ready for the chloral hydrate and a wet sheet by that time.

As I looked for a cab, I added up the interview. Pack had undoubtedly seen or dodged—which could have been significant too—Johnny Mallo on Friday night. He was in love with Lorry. He had recognized Sam Fenner's name.

Also, Ralph Pack was not to be underestimated. I had made an intelligent, tough, and, possibly, desperate enemy. The extent of his interference with my activities would be limited only by the extent of his involvement in Mallo's death.

Most importantly, I came to the conclusion that the physician either knew it had been murder or thought it was. I got a sudden desire to see Lorry Mallo. It was only a little after nine, and my Sunday-night call to Katie would leave me free by nine-thirty.

I phoned Lorry when I got home. She was pleasant enough—brightening up considerably when I told her I might have something of importance to offer on the subject of her insurance. She said come any time.

My long-distance call was completed almost at once. Katie was up-tempo and chattery. "Jimmy, darling! Isn't this wonderful! How is Sauki-no-no?"

Sauki-no-no! Is that nice? "I'm very well, thank you. So good of you to inquire."

"You're spoiled. We'll start again. How are you, dear?"

"Very well, thanks—considering—"

"Considering what?"

"Considering my activities. But it's nice to have so much to keep me busy while you're away. By the time I've thawed food and done my chambermaiding in the morning—oh yes—and administered the brewer's yeast and the B complex *and* the cod-liver oil, I have a feeling of accomplishment; the strong knowledge that the world must be a better place, somehow, because I have lived and labored in it for those few, busy—"

"*Will* you shut up? What about the daily brushing?"

"I keep forgetting it."

"That's all right. She can't get too bad in two weeks. How about her elimination?"

"I haven't given it a serious thought since she jumped on my shoulder. I'm actually getting fond of her."

"You know what I mean, dammit! Physiologically. Is she eliminating properly? You have to watch that in cats all the time."

"The answer is yes to everything. She is eliminating properly—and continually. I'm thinking of subscribing to another newspaper."

"Thank you, darling. You're wonderful to take care of her! Did she actually jump on your shoulder?"

"Indeed she did—and damned near scared me to death. She also has learned to stalk up and down my spine of an early morning—"

"She *must* be fond of you! Now you're taking care of yourself, aren't you? Eating properly and picking your things up?"

"Sure I am. I'm swell. But listen, Katie, I miss you so terribly—it's pretty awful—"

"I miss you, too, Jimmy—achingly. And I worry about you. I keep thinking about how much trouble you can get yourself into sometimes—you know what I mean. I want you to promise—"

"I'm perfectly all right. Can't we talk about you for—"

"I want you to promise not to do anything *silly;* anything like playing cops 'n robbers with Eddie Marsh and getting shot at. Or your leg broken, like you did before. Will you promise?"

I don't know what they're proving down at Duke University with playing cards, but if they had Katie for a day or two, they could write the last chapter and go home. She's got extra-sensory perception over the phone; I didn't have time to think up anything before she was after me. "Doc! You've—oh, *no,* darling!"

"It's just a little one. No shooting or anything. Eddie doesn't even think it *is* one. It's only an idea of mine—"

"That's awful! I never should have left New York. It's even worse than if it was a *real* one and Eddie was along with his gun and everything. You shouldn't have ideas about murders by yourself, and you know it! Are you in any danger yet?"

"None at all. It isn't like that, you see. It's simply a case where a man—"

"That's good, dear. You must take care of yourself. I've been watching my sweep second hand and it's coming up time, now, so I'll hang up."

"But *Katie!* I haven't even had a chance to—"

"You shouldn't be so extravagant on the long-distance phone. Good night, darling."

Oh, Katie, Katie, Katie!

9

I headed for the Mallo apartment, restless as a drying drunk. Broadway was full of Sunday-evening strollers. They didn't have any place to go either, only they didn't give a damn. They didn't have to dig up facts for Eddie Marsh.

What I'd got from Ralph Pack was all implication. What I was on my way to get from Lorry would be no better. Marsh has always said that murder without evidence-physical evidence—is a pipe dream. Where was the evidence?

Not in Mallo's body, signed Crane, M.D., Ph.D. Maybe where the body had been? Maybe in the reducing cabinet? The room itself? Yes—a hunch, signed James Cardigan Connor, M.D., period.

I got considerably more interested in my trip all at once.

Lorry Mallo was very pleasant. There was cigar smoke in her living room, but no stump in evidence. The remains of two drinks messed up the coffee table.

"You were good to let me come so late, Lorry. I hope I didn't drive anyone away."

She smiled. "No. I did. The subject you mentioned over the phone sounded rather more important. Please sit down."

"I haven't too much time. If you don't object, I'd like to take a look at the cabinet again. I'm not absolutely certain, but there's a reasonable chance that we've overlooked something—a possibility."

"The possibility of an accident?"

"Yes. Could be. It's something that should have occurred to any of us—but didn't, for some reason. You realize, of course, that the bathroom is one of the commonest places for accidents—including fatal ones?"

She alerted immediately, interested and hopeful. "You mean from slipping and—things like that?"

"Not slipping in this case. The medical examination eliminates that almost positively. I mean death from electric shock."

She was in there at once, pitching for all that dough. "Oh! I've heard of things like that—accidents. Electric heaters and lights. People touch them while they're in bathtubs and—"

"That's right. There were two hundred and twenty volts in that cabinet—twice the voltage that's used in most house-lighting circuits."

"I remember the man who installed the sweatbox saying that it would add too much load or something to the rest of the apartment."

"Exactly. I want to examine that switch, Lorry. If there's anything wrong with it, Johnny's death would—or, rather, need—not be a mystery any longer."

"And that would be an accident, of course—the sort of an accident the insurance company would have to accept?"

"Yes. I think it would be." I couldn't resist adding, "Double indemnity, naturally." I watched for things to happen in the sapphire eyes. They did. "May I go back and look around?"

"Please do. I'm afraid the place is a mess. I haven't had the—courage to go in there again."

"Of course not!" I got up and started across the room. She showed no indication of wanting to follow me, but I played it safe. "Lorry, if anyone comes to the door while I'm back there, stall long enough for me to get out. I want to avoid the appearance of conspiracy. It's very important. That would be the first thing the insurance company would try to prove."

"Oh. Yes, I see that." She sat thoughtful for an instant. Then, "Someone could do things to the switch—afterward, couldn't they?"

"Sure. I won't be long." I went down the narrow hall to the reducing room and turned on the big light.

Everything looked exactly as Eddie Marsh and I had last seen it. There wouldn't be much reason to hide what had been left there—no weapon, no fingerprints that would be worth anything. I went over the story in my mind again, and ended up where I'd been before—if there were any evidence of a physical nature, it had to be here.

Johnny hadn't left much behind, poor little guy—the smell of rubdown, Bigeloil, used by horses and horsemen alike, a battered old exposure timer, a wrinkled towel with the print of his bony, saddle-pounded prat still in it. Not much else.

There was an inch or so of water left where he'd had his feet. The gauze bandage lay, as it had, under the table. Nothing of all this was *part* of him. They were the things he *used* and *did* and *wore*.

He'd left behind only the man-killing, hard-earned pounds that had once been the fluid and tissue of his lean body.

I started an inch-by-inch search of the bare room looking for something—maybe only an idea. Nothing in the shower; A drawer in the rubbing table held two bars of unwrapped soap, a couple of half-empty rubdown bottles, and some shaving tack.

I turned to the cabinet, put on the heating lights, stuck my left hand in the foot bath, and slapped the switch housing a couple of times. No shock. No accident, anyway. It could have been shorted and repaired, of course. I spent some time wondering whether, if I'd electrocuted a man in that sweatbox, I'd have repaired the short.

After ten or fifteen minutes of poring over the cabinet, I was glad to pull my head out of the sweaty odor. I sat back on the floor and gave up the search. The only thing Johnny hadn't taken with him to the autopsy was the gallon or so of sweat which cost him his life. I got to my feet with, the bitter thought that he should have carried it along—in a bucket. It was the only part of him, after all, which Storky Crane hadn't taken apart. It took about ten seconds for the idea to press any buttons, then all the bells went off at once!

First, a bottle. I hurried to the rubbing table and pulled the drawer out—all the way out—grabbed for the back end, and bounced my sore knuckles against the table. All the junk hit the deck, and the drawer landed upside down. There was a plain manila envelope taped to the bottom—an ancient device for hiding light, flat things. I carefully removed it, then, with care that amounted to reverence, replaced the whole mess exactly as I'd found it, except for the alcohol bottle.

The envelope held five very new, very handsome thousand-dollar bills!

But that, as the feller said, is the way it goes. Within a minute after I'd decided the party was over, I had a definitely first-class murder method, plus a motive that a Ubangi could understand!

I rinsed the bottle a dozen times at the sink and did a thorough job at cleaning the screw top. Then I swabbed down the sides of the foot bath with a clean handkerchief to catch any crystals left by evaporation. Then I filled the bottle.

The towel which had been on the chair I wrapped around my waist, under my coat. There would be crystallized material in that too. I think it was a sort of joke I'd made on the phone to Katie, that evening, that made me start thinking about what might be hidden in those crystals—a joke about Sauki-no-no.

I stuck the bottle into my pocket and went back to the living room. Lorry was at the telephone. She spoke quickly and softly as I entered, then hung up. It needn't have meant anything. Could have been a report to Pack.

She turned without apparent self-consciousness. "What did you find, Doc? Was there anything wrong with the switch?"

"I can't tell exactly. I'm not very expert at electricity." It wouldn't hurt to keep the switch gag going awhile. "The lights seem to go on and off well enough. Of course I didn't try it with my feet in the water. That would be pretty risky, even for a man who's expecting it."

"Maybe we should have it looked into tomorrow. By an electrician."

"Maybe we should. If you'll call me in the morning, I'll fix it up for you."

"Thanks so much." I saw her staring at the bulge in my pocket. "You've been very kind."

I hastened to explain the bulge. "By the way, just to be sure I haven't overlooked any possibility, I'm taking along a bottle of rubbing alcohol Johnny had been using. I'd like to see that it's all right. It was the only thing around that might have had anything like poison in it."

She wasn't disturbed. "Of course, Doc. Anything you say."

I got my hat and made a couple of departing gestures before I said what I'd been waiting to say. Lorry followed me to the door muttering small variations on the theme of gratitude. I let her think I was on my way, then, "Did Johnny have a habit of keeping a lot of money around the apartment?"

I got a puzzled look for my strategy, nothing more. "Money?"

"Yes. Maybe quite large sums."

"Like—how much?" I think she meant it without guile.

"Enough to justify a rather desperate attempt to get it—like several thousand dollars."

She shook her head. "You didn't know Johnny, Doc. He's never carried more than ten dollars in his life. He was always hustling me for a dollar or two out of my household money. As far as keeping that kind of money around the place—" She shrugged her shoulders.

"We've never given much thought to the possibility of robbery, you know. I just wondered—" I backed out into the hall. Lorry made a gesture toward me with her hand. I said, "It might have been that way if Johnny had made some sort of a deal—received a sum of money, for instance, where other people could see it. Somebody might have slipped in while he was in the back room. That sort of thing happens."

"Doc, have you any—reason—to believe my husband had been carrying a large sum of, money on Friday night?"

"None at all, and since you say he never kept such sums in the house, I suppose we can just charge it off as another good theory all shot. You know you have to keep trying everything."

"Do keep trying, won't you, Doc?"

I patted her on the back, keeping it as avuncular as I could. "Don't worry, youngster. We'll stay at it until we land you something better than that benefit you've been worrying about."

And why shouldn't she worry? A telephone switchboard may be a dandy way to make a living, but not too nice to come back to after you've been sprung from it for four years. At least I could surprise her with five thousand lovely dollars she seemed not to know about. Unless somebody beat me to it.

On my way home I nursed some doubts about leaving the money there. Maybe I should have substituted a statement to the effect that I had removed it for safekeeping and considered it a sacred trust. Or maybe I should have left a ninety-day note and bought myself a custom-made British roadster I'd seen. Yellow. I got tired of walking and whistled down a cab. Also yellow. It had been a large Sunday.

10

I woke up Monday morning baying like a hound—full of purpose and investigative determination. I bounced Sauki-no-no off my back, thawed her food, did my housework, grabbed the towel and the bottle, and headed for Harry Welker's laboratory.

Harry is afflicted with exophthalmos and a compulsive curiosity to take things apart and see what they're made of. He's a thick-lensed witch doctor with no more respect for imagination than an I.B.M. sorting machine. He came out of the big back room with all the cordiality of an Airedale interrupted in the middle of a meal. After peering at me he said, "Oh. Hello, Doc."

"Hi, Harry." I lugged out my bottle and put it on the counter. "Here's something. I want to find out what's in it."

Welker grunted. "That's a big order. You'd better limit your instructions a little—or else endow the place. What're you looking for?"

"Damned if I know, exactly. It's water and sweat." I got the towel out of a paper bag. "This'll be more of the same—crystallized. A guy sat on this and died—sweat his life away—with his feet in what's in the bottle. There wasn't any reason for it as far as the autopsy showed. I've a hunch that, if he left any evidence behind at all, it'll be here."

"Oh. The jockey—what's his name?"

"Johnny Mallo."

"I was interested in the newspaper accounts. Not many deaths from dehydration—at least not from causes like artificial heat."

"That's right. It's a puzzler."

"Nothing in the papers to imply any crime—"

"That's right. The police aren't interested—yet."

Harry grinned. I think that's what he did. It's hard to tell. "Up to your old tricks, eh, Doc?"

"I'm afraid so, Harry. When can you give me a report?"

He pulled off his glasses and scratched the back of his neck with one of the bows. "I don't think I'd even bother to try chemical analysis on a solution like this. It's a spectroscopic job, I'd say." He put the cheaters on again.

"When?"

"Your curiosity eating on you?"

"Devouring me."

"So's mine. I'll call you late this afternoon sometime."

He got a wired tag and a gummed label which he attached to the towel and the bottle. "Better mark these, Doc. If I know you, they'll be in court one of these days." He handed me a fountain pen and I wrote dates, source, and my signature on each. I noticed the towel bore an MAL laundry mark. Welker added dates and initials of his own.

I left him bearing our prizes back into the Temple of the Test Tubes.

The next call was one I should have made earlier in the game—like Saturday afternoon. I rode the subway to Kew Gardens, took a cab to the track, talked my way into the stable-area gate, and went to the jock house.

It was midmorning but the Professor was about. The Professor, in case you haven't heard of him, won his name from two generations of riders for whom he has prescribed diet, supervised, reducing baths, rubbed the bruises out of, and generally counseled. He's built along lines that suggest he may have assumed for his own use most of the pounds he'd taken off the boys—a big, good-natured man with plenty of savvy about his specialty. He hollered down the stairs for me to come up to his office—a little cubbyhole next to the shower room.

I joined him and squeezed into the extra chair. The walls were covered with photographs of riders whose names stirred memories. "Well, Doc, it's good to meet you. I heard a lot about you from my kids."

"I know quite a few of them pretty well, Professor."

The big guy chuckled. "They remember you mostly from around the barns—like doctorin' horses' legs. At the track here they say you're the best man in the business on gimpy legs."

"I've been around horses all my life. I enjoy working with them."

He looked up a little shyly. "You'd think you'd do more of it—if you'll pardon my sayin' so. They's always room for a first-class vet."

"But I'm not a veterinarian, you see. That does make a difference after all, Professor."

"You're a *human* doctor?"

"Very."

"Oh! I'm sorry, Doc, I—"

"So am I, sometimes, Professor." We both did a touch of friendly grinning. "That's one of the things I want to talk to you about—some human-doctoring problems I can't figure out."

"Land sakes! If you can't figure 'em out, I certainly can't. All the doctorin' I know is just the little stuff I do for the riders."

"That's what I want to know about. You've probably had more experience in weight control, for instance, than any man in America."

The Professor looked pleased and squirmy. "Well, I don't know about that, but I'll tell you anything I can, Doc."

"Good. You've worked with Johnny Mallo, haven't you?"

"Since he started—poor little feller. He's had a rough time makin' weight this last year or two. I tried to warn him a dozen times not to take them light-weighted horses." He looked up to the wall and pointed. "There he is, right up there." There was a piece of black crepe paper on the picture. He shook his head. "You know, I hate to say it after he's dead and all that, but the boy acted to me like he was money hungry. He took every mount he could get—weight or no weight."

"Johnny had a very expensive wife, I suspect."

"You aren't just kiddin'. I seen her around." With this went a chubby and not unpleasant leer. "What you want to know about Johnny, Doc?"

"Something about his reducing habits. I know he had his own equipment, but did you advise him on his routine?"

"I taught the boy everything he knew about reducing—from his first season on. I can't understand what happened to him. It had to be a heart attack, didn't it?"

"Look, Professor, you've been around a long time, and you've learned to keep your own counsel—to keep things to yourself—"

"I sure have. Why, man, I've listened to more personal troubles—"

"That's what I mean. I want a lot of help from you, and I've got to trust you with something that may turn out to be just a very nasty idea. I don't think it will. Will you help me on that basis?"

"Why, sure I will. I wasn't too fond of the boy, when you get right down to it, but he was one of my kids. I'll help you in any way I can, Doc."

"All right—and thanks. It wasn't a heart attack, Professor. His heart was as sound as a bell o' brass the night he died."

"Land sakes! What'd he do? Just set in that sweatbox and cook himself to death?"

"That's about it. He—went to sleep."

"*No,* sir! He never *stayed* asleep after he begun to get real uncomfortable. The boys snooze in the baths all the time. I've watched them for thirty years. Then they wake up and holler for me to turn 'em out long before it's time. Johnny done it like they all do, I can even remember him *doin'* it."

"That's one of the things I wanted to be sure about. Now, what did he do, as a rule, in each step of the bath—getting ready for it and all?"

"Excuse me, Doc, but from the way you talk, I'd say you think somebody may have *done* something to him."

"I do, Professor—pretty much for the reasons you've just mentioned." The round face looked shocked, incredulous. He started to say something and thought better of it. I got the quick hunch he was about to tell me of the bitterness between Johnny and Mickey. But Mickey was one of his boys too. He stared at the wall over my head. I wondered if Mick's picture was up there.

"For the last couple of years, as I say, Johnny's been having trouble making weight. He was forced to stay too long in the box and was losing too much energy along with the weight. It would take quite a while in the heat before he'd even begin to break out in a sweat, and that helped weaken him. Well, about a year and a half ago I started him to taking a double hooker of some kind of bonded whisky and a big cup of very sweet chocolate—good and hot—about ten minutes before he started his bath."

"The liquor and heat to start the perspiration—"

"That's right, and the sweetened chocolate for quick energy, without laying on fat like starches." I didn't argue. Mine was from the book—his from the scales.

"Did Johnny drink much otherwise?"

"Not at all—that I know of. It was strictly off his diet of course. A race rider can't drink steady and make weight."

"How long would he usually stay in the cabinet, Professor?"

"That depends on if he'd had a few idle days—which he didn't, too often. When he was at one thirteen or so, half an hour or thirty-five minutes should have been enough."

Things began to fall together, finally, in my head. A shrill young voice hollered outside for the Professor. He started to rise, and I told him I had to hurry away, thanked him, and beat it.

A double hooker of whisky and a big cup of thick, hot chocolate!

As I rumbled home in the subway, I resisted the thoughts which beset me as well as I could—pending Harry Welker's findings. The one thought I couldn't crowd out, though, was that I'd liked to have made a little bet on what he would find.

When I got to the apartment, Mrs. Parter was there, and the place looked like a rummage sale. Mrs. Parter is a staunch and disapproving friend who, in addition to seeing, personally, to the cleanliness of several public buildings near by, swamps my place out once a week. She's nothing if not vigorous and takes the joint apart on each occasion. She informed me over the screaming of the vacuum cleaner that she had the cat locked in the bedroom and that—here, I've got it wrote down—Mrs. Mallo wanted me to come over at once. The call had come only a few minutes before.

I hurriedly put Sauki-no-no's pan and water in with her, and dashed off for the Mallo apartment. Lorry met me at the door with import and revelation written all over her pretty face.

"Oh, Doc! Come in! I'm so glad you got here in time!" She hustled me into the living room. "I've been trying to reach you." There was a guy standing there in overalls. He had screw driver and wire cutter in his jeans, and I gave myself a silent *oh*-oh. Lorry said, "This is the electrician, Doc; he says there's something the matter with the switch."

"I see. What was the matter with the switch, mister?"

"Like I told the lady, it would've been dangerous. Could easy have blown the circuit or even hurt somebody. I pulled the main before I took the cover off the switch or I might've gotten it myself."

"What was wrong with it?"

"Why, they was a piece of the housing insulation tore away—I don't think I done it when I opened it up—and one side of the circuit was loose on the binding post."

"Would the cabinet lights go on and off?"

"How would anybody find out? I wasn't going to throw the main after I seen the condition the switch was in. That's just askin' for trouble!"

"Did you fix the switch?"

"No. The lady said I should wait until somebody else saw it."

Lorry had stood quietly during the colloquy. She said, "Don't you think I was right, Doctor? It solves the whole problem!"

I turned to the electrician. "You charge by the hour?"

"Yeah. By the hour. From the time I leave the shop."

"You wouldn't mind waiting a few minutes then? This dangerous condition you found in the switch may be the landlord's carelessness. Between you and me, this, lady is anxious to break her lease, and this looks like her chance. Will you wait?"

"Sure. It's nothin' to me. Besides, any landlord who'd let his stuff get in shape like that *ought* to lose his lease. I'll go back and look it over again. I'll have to fix the switch before I go, though—unless you wanta leave the main switch off."

Lorry said, "Don't do anything to it until the—the other people see it. That's very important."

The electrician mumbled something and left. The girl turned to me with an expression of puzzled innocence.

"That's right—isn't it, Doc? The insurance people should see it?"

"I hope not."

"I don't understand. Why shouldn't the insurance people see it?" A little too challenging. "Now we know it was an accident."

"It was a murder, Lorry, and you'd better use your head from here on in. I think I'll know by tonight how someone killed your husband, and I'm not saying anything more until I do. You'd better have the man fix up the switch—right now. Then you'd better forget it."

"You think that I—*did* something to the switch?"

"Yes. At least somebody did. It was all right last night. I checked it."

"But, Doc! You said—"

"I know what I said. Listen to me, Lorry. Making murders look like accidents is routine procedure with killers—and not for insurance money either. Get off the dime, youngster, and behave yourself, or you'll be the number one suspect by tomorrow."

She said nothing—sat down and looked out the window. I tramped about the room wondering if somebody had helped her do that bungling job on the wiring. Whoever did it could certainly be eliminated from any electrocution theory. As a gesture—a demonstration of electrical innocence—it would have been just too shrewd for most of the people concerned. I marched back to Lorry.

"Look; just because you—or you and somebody else—did this silly thing is no sign I believe you murdered your husband.

It's stupid and it—complicates things. Forget it. I'm going to."

She looked a little frightened, but that dough had her by the throat. "But, Doc; the insurance company—"

"Goddammit, Lorry, the insurance company will throw you in the can for attempted fraud. How the hell do you expect to tear pieces of lining out of a switch box—leave fresh screw-driver marks in the metal—and get away with it! The moment a piece of protected metal is exposed to the air it's like setting a time clock. I know guys who could tell you within an hour of when it was done. Now go tell that electrician to fix the switch. I've got a date with a chemist."

She stood up slowly. "All right. I'll tell him." She'd let down badly. "I don't know how I should thank you—"

"Don't thank me. Just don't try to confuse this thing any more. Keep that beautiful nose clean and wait it out. So long, Lorry."

As I left, I saw her plugging down the long hall toward the room where Johnny Mallo had died.

In the cab going home I kept thinking about Ralph Pack-Pack and Lorry. If Harry Welker came up with the answer I expected, I'd have to turn Eddie Marsh loose on the man.

Mrs. Parter had finished up and left. There was a note collared around the neck of the Forester bottle. Call Dr. Welker. I went to the telephone feeling like a candidate waiting for election returns. Somebody at the laboratory hollered for Harry and he came on. "Hi, Doc."

"What you got, Harry?"

"Want to guess?"

"Want to bet?"

"No. Once you had the facts, a good cook could have figured it. Did your jockey go to sleep in the bath?"

"That makes more sense than anything. Now you know why, eh?"

"Right. Unless somebody's doing a hell of a scientific job kidding you, he went to sleep. I've got positive indication—spectroscopically, of course, of *sodium ethyl (1-methylbutyl) barbiturate.* It apparently wasn't a massive dose."

"It wouldn't have to be." I thanked him and hung up—with the murder method neatly in my mind and one word in my ears.

Nembutal!

I dutifully reported to Eddie. He gave me an argument, of course. "You're nuts! How the hell could Mallo have been drugged? Storky Crane's report—"

"Forget Crane's report for a minute and listen. Mallo didn't have any drugs in him when Crane worked on the body. He'd eliminated the drug."

"How?"

"Sweat, Eddie. Nembutal is easily eliminated through the skin. That's one of the reasons it's so useful."

"Did it kill him?"

"No. It did the same thing for him as it does for anybody else—helped him into a deep sleep. He died from dehydration—as advertised—but a reducing bath is a hell of a place to take a four- or five-hour nap."

"So there was nothing for them to find at the autopsy."

"Actually there was. They didn't look in the right place. Tell Harry Welker to get over to the undertaker's and take some spongings from the skin. If they haven't washed the body too thoroughly he should find enough."

Eddie said he'd be damned, and hung up. He would have been quite a lot damneder if I hadn't held out on him about the light switch, Elegant Johnson, and the five grand.

11

Tuesday and Thursday mornings bring what Katie hopefully calls The Clinic. It started by accident and has been continued as a palliative for my conscience. At least it keeps the queen-of-love-and-beauty and Marsh mollified—although Eddie occasionally refers to me as a minor-league Mayo.

By nine o'clock on each of these gruesome days the waiting room is crawling with local citizenry. I have a sneaking hunch that I do more business per square foot than some of the other free clinics around town, because my place is nearer at hand. Perhaps, more importantly, because it's nearly always good for a laugh. Clubby.

I wiped the egg off and headed through to my office. It sounded like the floor of the Stock Exchange from the outside. It would be a one-o'clock day—maybe later. Johnny Mallo's funeral was at two. There was a baby howling. I stuck my head out. "Good morning. Let's take the baby first—then come in order as usual. Get that straightened out right now too. I refuse to referee any more brawls about who's next."

It turned out to be a one-thirty day which went into the books as something of a record—not one hangover, and the old cigar box in my desk remained intact. Everybody seemed to have money enough to fill prescriptions. I made a note to consult the financial section and see whether there had been a national boom which had escaped my attention.

I grabbed some quick bad hash at Rosie's and cabbed over to the Tanniger Funeral Home. Harry Welker was just walking out of the place carrying a small square case.

"Hi, Harry? See you heard from Marsh. Get what you wanted?"

"I suppose so, Doc. I called here last night and told them what to do. I've got spongings—axillary and general surface. If the samples you brought me were out of this fellow, I've probably got something."

"Good. That's where we want to find it. Ties it up. Let me know, will you, Harry?"

The guy actually blushed. It took him something beyond the human interval but he made it. "Well—I'd be glad to, Doc, only—"

"Did that lug tell you not to give me anything?" Eddie Marsh was reverting to type again, and I didn't like it

"Not exactly. He wants it kept quiet. That's why he called me—I already knew about it. He's apparently got some sort of deal on with his boss—"

"Deal, hell! I just gave him some facts that scared him to death. He didn't dare ask the department to do this job for fear he'd get laughed out of the place."

Welker started a retreat. "I know nothing about it, Doc. I'm sure they'll be glad to—"

"I'm sure they will, Harry. So long."

He hurried down the street and I went on into the undertaker's place. It was complete with sunshine and canaries. A small chapel opened off to the right of the hall, and a hired hand mourned me in. The room, was more than half full, and I recognized a number of faces. Frank Latch sat with Jimmy Ferry, Johnny's agent, and the Professor. A couple of sports writers walked out past me for a last drag on the porch. Several riders had given up their afternoon's work to see Johnny off. No principals yet.

The casket was in the front of the chapel with a lot of flowers banked around it. No horseshoes. I sat in a rear corner near the door.

Ralph Pack appeared and the organ gave him a doleful salute and accompanied him down to a seat near the front He settled himself and, for a moment, bowed his head. I suspected it was to see that his striped trousers weren't being stretched at the knees. A nasty turn of mind.

Huck Trask walked in and looked around for Eve. She hurried through the door and breezed past me, leaving a delicate
trail of apple blossom and applejack. I might have been mistaken about the apple blossom. They fooled around the aisle,
nodded to Pack, and sat down next to him. There wasn't much
choice after they'd committed themselves that far forward in
the chapel. The only other pew, directly across, was roped off.

A man who'd been stationed up front in a corner, intently
watching the rear, nodded briefly, and made a sign with his
gloved hand in acknowledgment of some silent instruction. He
moved forward to the family pew, took down the white cord,
and stood, sympathetic and understanding, as Lorry came down
the aisle with Mickey leaning on her arm. The man's eyes widened visibly as he took his first look at the widow. I guess that's
the way things are.

So there they were—all lined up in a neat row. Murderer's
Row. I counted off the backs of their heads and wondered what
was going on in them. There were a lot of hot, primitive drives
lashing about under those well-groomed skulls—up and down
those well-clothed spinal ganglia. Lust, greed, fear, hatred—solid, murderous patterns since the beginnings. The fact that they
were housed in broadcloth and satin instead of skins changed
them not at all—simply darkened them with cunning.

A clear, gently lyric tenor began to sing "Just As I Am,
Without One Plea." I looked up and found him standing by the
organ. Damned if it wasn't Red Morrissey, a veteran jock and
a good one. A blue suit and a brave white carnation dignified
his modest fame for warbling Irish ballads around the track. I
looked again at my five-in-a-line suspects and wondered if one
of them could have suggested the simple hymn to which I had
been baptized.

The minister spoke feelingly—referring to his notes when
he had to recall the name of the deceased brother.

All in all, it was one of the four-hundred-ninety-five-dollar
package jobs, and you couldn't expect much. The pallbearers
turned out to be the group of riders I'd seen, and Johnny went
out of there about eighteen inches off the floor.

I waited until Lorry and Mickey had disappeared through the door, and beat most of the crowd out; ducked headlong down the street to Lexington where I could find a hack. I felt lousy. Rosie's sodden hash was annoying me, and I needed a drink. The cab tacked across town and dumped me in front of Gallagher's. It was too early, but the boss was sitting at the end of the bar working on some papers. He looked up and said, "Hello, Doc. Come in."

The barman slipped on his white jacket. "What'll it be, Doctor—bourbon old-fashioned?"

"Old-fashioned bourbon—leave out the sugar, bitters, and salad."

Without raising his head the boss said, "What? No double?"

"Sure. A double. Sorry—I was confusing myself with somebody else."

Sure. Make it a double shot of some kind of good bonded whisky. Follow it with four or five grains of Nembutal in hot, sweet chocolate—a big cup. Be sure to make it Elixir of Nembutal, bartender. That's a liquid. It even tastes a little like chocolate. Your—customer won't notice the alcohol in the elixir because he's just had his whisky. The drink will help him sweat *quickly*. The *Nembutal* will help him sweat *comfortably*—until he's dead. Then, when he's dead, he'll get a nice, second-rate funeral—

I gulped my drink and walked home. I had a murder. Suicide was out. It was silly to think that Mallo would have destroyed himself by a process he'd come to hate and dread. I felt certain, too, that he would have known too much about the fine print on his insurance policies to obscure his finish.

I called Marsh from the apartment.

"That was a nice job of work, Doc."

"What's the idea of shutting off on me?"

"I don't get you."

"The hell you don't! I met Harry Welker at the undertaker's."

"Oh. That." He might have been a little embarrassed. "I'll tell you, Doc, this thing you've dug up makes it tricky. I don't know what I've got yet. The quantitative analysis—"

"I know what you've got!" I must have hollered because I heard him laugh. It made me sorer than ever. "You've got the bull by the tail! You've got your pants down. You've got the record full of the autopsy findings and you've—"

"Hold it, will you?" His tone was such that I held it. "Those autopsy findings are going to break the case, Doc. You haven't seen it, of course, but there's a lot of stuff that might make you change your mind—"

That tamed me down a little. "You gave me the essential facts, didn't you?"

"That's right. The facts that seemed essential then."

"So. Mallo had to have been given the stuff sometime not earlier than maybe nine-thirty. That gives you half an hour to work on. During that half hour he was with Eve Trask—he was with Ralph Pack—he was with—"

"Mickey and Huck Trask—"

"*What?*"

"That's right. It may be something, but I doubt it. I'll tell you about it. I let the routine go as far as placing the people." He chuckled softly—which is a low, animal growl. "But you were saying—"

"All right, dammit! I was saying that he saw those people and his wife—all within the thirty minutes in which he must have gotten the drug."

"O.K., kid. Forgive the ribbing. You get so damned opinionated that I can't help it. You got it all right except one thing. I'd better tell you. We have no idea, whatever, when Mallo went into that bath. We picked that up in the routine."

I was still spluttering when he said, "Lorry Mallo was with a woman friend on Long Island; at the movies and a local pub. First time she saw Mallo was at three-fifteen in the morning. He was dead. She was afraid the insurance company—or Pack—might think she was negligent or something."

"But when she needs a first-class killing to get her dough, she comes through with her alibi!"

"Completely correct. Hell, Doc! You can't blame the kid—"

I thought of the hundred and fifty grand—and the benefit. "I suppose not." Then, "Look, Eddie, did Trask and Mickey tell you what they talked with Johnny about—why he was there?"

"No. There was no reason to push them. Why?"

"I think I know what it was, and I think there was a hell of a lot of cash money involved. Maybe our Johnny wasn't as nice a guy as I thought."

"What would that make?"

"That would make a tremendous lot of sense. Let Trask alone—and Mickey, too—until I beat the truth out of one of them."

"You start beating the truth or anything else out of anybody and I'll throw you in—"

My turn to laugh. "Figuratively, chum, figuratively. There's a little matter of a horse called Nautilus I want to talk to them about. They'll be very touchy on the subject." I felt good; excited and certain. Lorry's presence in the apartment had limited my thinking. The ten-o'clock deadline was off, and anything could have happened. "I'll find a weak spot within twenty-four hours."

"You'll find a shive in your ribs too." Marsh growled. The rhythmic pound would be his fist on the desk. "How many times do I have to remind you that I've finally earned myself a nice, quiet desk job? I don't even carry a gun any more. I'm absolutely through running into corners and shooting people to pull you out of holes. We'll have pleasant, orderly talks with everybody and compare their statements. If they disagree, we'll compare their disagreements. Sooner or later we'll have a case against the right one. You stay out of trouble. I'll see you maybe tomorrow."

That again! From the beginning of our association, Marsh has posed as boon companion just long enough to get all the meat of a case out of me—then turned cop on me. Sure he's pulled me out of some holes! But he never found me in a spot like that when I didn't have my teeth sunk in the hind leg of a killer—except a lady one once.

I was reeking with resentment when the telephone rang. It was Lorry Mallo. "Doc! I haven't been able to call you before. The place has been full of people—making me lie down and cooking things for me. I've been losing my mind!"

"What's the trouble?"

"Somebody broke into the apartment last night, searched things. I'm terrified—"

"Tell me about it."

"I couldn't stand it here and went out—"

"Where?"

"It doesn't make any difference." Impatiently. "Let me tell you. When I got home around ten-thirty I heard someone in the back of the house. Footsteps. I thought it was Mickey and called out. The footsteps hurried without trying to be quiet, and someone went through the kitchen window down the fire escape. They'd been searching Johnny's bureau. One of the drawers was standing open and the rest of them were a mess. I'm getting out of here—"

"What could they have been looking for?"

"I haven't any idea."

"You think they were in the bedroom when you came in?"

"I'm sure of it."

"Then whoever it was didn't get what he wanted. He'll be back."

"He won't find me—I—"

"You didn't report it to the police?"

"Of course not. It could have been Mick—I'm sure Johnny had something of his. Besides, I was afraid I'd—complicate things."

I thought of Marsh and his pleasant, orderly talks. "Maybe you were right, Lorry. You said you were going somewhere?"

"I am, within ten minutes. I'm going to visit a woman friend on Long Island."

I let it go. "Would you like me to stick around the apartment tonight—just in case?"

"Oh—I'd appreciate it tremendously, Doc. I can fix it with the manager so you can get in any time."

"Good. Do that. Tell me; did your intruder search the reducing room?"

"No. That was curious, wasn't it!"

"How do you know he didn't? Incidentally, why was it curious?"

"I pegged a pin in the floor—I thought somebody might—"

"Tamper with the switch?"

"That's cruel! You know how important it is to me—"

"I guess it was a little cruel. But the switch idea made you think you didn't want anybody monkeying around in there?"

"That's just it. I half expected someone might want to—make trouble for me."

"Who?"

She hesitated. "Huck Trask."

"Huck Trask? Why?"

"He called me last night—threatened me. I didn't know what he was talking about, but he wouldn't believe me."

"What did he say?"

"He said Johnny had something that belonged to him and that I knew what it was: a sealed envelope with his—Huck's—name on it—"

"Did you ever see such an envelope?"

"Never. But Huck wouldn't believe me—asked me if Johnny had said anything about giving it to you—"

"Me? Why would he have given it to me?"

"I don't know. He just said that. Then he got mad and told me that if I didn't get it for him, he'd make trouble for me."

"What sort of trouble?"

"Just trouble." She sobbed a couple of quick ones, then said, "Money trouble!"

I settled the arrangement about the manager and excused myself.

12

Now it's intruders, threats, and missing envelopes!

The little widow had manufactured one accident with nothing but an idea and a screw driver. Fashioning a suspicion of murder and hanging it on Huck Trask seemed a trifle complicated but strictly in character. Why hadn't she fled to Pack with her tale of dark deeds?

I'd been so kind about the light switch. Maybe I'd be good enough to laugh this one off if I didn't think it would work— even if she had held out a neat packet of five new thousand-dollar bills that belonged to Trask in the process.

Maybe, also, the girl was telling the truth and I was getting some posts in my fence—the couple of facts I needed to beat Marsh over the head with.

I was weighing that with the idea of red herring in general when the herring idea overtook me, fished around in my associations, and came up with Lindy's. I put on my fine city suit and strolled over. It was early and there was room between the public figures. My dinner was a considerable cut over Rosie's hash and altogether reportable to Katie.

Thus fortified, I hailed a cab and rode over to the Mallo apartment building. I rang the manager and was admitted to the lobby by a little man with small, bright eyes set close to a sharp nose. Birdy little guy.

"I'm Dr. Connor. Did Mrs. Mallo tell you about me?"

"She said you would be in. Have you some sort of identification?"

I showed him some stuff from my wallet. "May I ask if this is routine? Or is it something special?"

He twittered, snapped his beak at me. "Both, Doctor. A very proper routine *and,* in this case, very special, also. After all, the police were here on Saturday morning and there have been other—irregularities."

"Other irregularities? Like what?"

He fixed me with his brittle eyes. "I know very little about the circumstances of Mr. Mallo's death, sir, but if it had happened on *Thursday* night instead of Friday—"

I added to his bitterness by refusing to be drawn out. "May I go up now, please?"

The little man shrugged like a saint worn with striving and marched off to the elevator, his heels ringing out his annoyance. As we rode up he said, "Will you be long, Doctor? Perhaps there is something I—"

"Thanks. I won't need you. I may be here most of the night."

"Oh?" He spent quite a lot of time saying it.

"If there's any objection I could call Lieutenant Marsh and ask for a police officer to stand by. It would relieve you of—"

"Not at all. Not at *all!* I merely wished to be helpful. You are to have complete freedom." He spread a wing to show the extent of my freedom and banged his hand on the cage. At the apartment door he gave me an owlish leer. "I judge, Doctor, that you do not wish anyone admitted during your visit?"

"On the contrary. I'm very anxious to see anyone who wants to get in. Show him every courtesy and don't tell him I'm here."

I went into the living room and bolted the door behind me, pulled down the shades throughout the apartment and anchored them securely with things like book ends and canned goods. The kitchen window leading to the fire escape I left open and unshaded.

Before I turned off the kitchen light I looked into some of the cupboards and found what I was expecting. There was cocoa, dextrose, and a fifth of bonded whisky—not Old Forester. I closed the door after me so that my lights wouldn't be seen from that direction. There would hardly be visitors by fire escape before it got completely dark.

The medicine cabinet—as do all such—revealed many things of small import, but no barbiturates. From the bathroom, I prowled the place inch by inch, starting with the reducing room. Lorry's pin was neatly in place, and I stuck it back in its hole, when I'd opened the door, to mark its location. The five grand was intact and, as nearly as I could make out, hadn't been disturbed. There was no name on the envelope, neither Huck Trask's nor anybody else's. If Lorry had hidden it, there wouldn't be. I left, pinning the door again.

The bureau drawers had been straightened up and showed nothing. I left the living-room desk for the last, digging into places like the Murphy bed, closets, and the backs of mirrors and pictures. I looked at the bottom of every drawer in the house. If the intruder came in again, I could save him a lot of trouble.

Then I turned off all the lights in the place, except the small reading lamp over the desk, and settled down to dig through the miscellany of papers stuffed into pigeonholes and drawers. I could make little out of them, except that most of them related to the Mallo economy, and that Johnny had been an inveterate hanger-onto of any useless scrap pertaining to his paying or receiving money. Lorry's training in the value of a buck—or a hundred and fifty thousand of them—had been come by honestly.

With all this, however, there wasn't a single record of tax payments, riding income, or bank deposits. I searched diligently for a safety-deposit key without success. The guy had probably had an accountant. I wondered, dimly, if it had been Huck Trask. Or Eve, whose blond head could easily contain a considerable amount of undisclosed wisdom.

It was a tempting premise on which to build a structure of falsified accounts, misappropriation of funds, and what not. If the relationships between these people were in any way strong—as Johnny's visits on the night of his death seemed to indicate—it would make sense to think they were a matter of business.

I filed the idea away for possible reference, snapped off the lamp, and groped my way across the unfamiliar terrain to the kitchen. It took a minute for my eyes to accommodate themselves to the darkness, then the window shaped itself before me, and the outline of the table below it fell into sketchy pieces where the reflection from the street touched vague highlights.

I listened. From outside and in the sounds were familiar— the passing cars, a woman calling someone in a loud voice while duller words drifted from open windows. I couldn't detach from these any sounds of stealth.

I crossed to the table and kneeled on it. It creaked. I leaned out and looked down the five floors of fire escape. There were crouching shadows on the landings below, but they repeated themselves, identically, on each level. I forced my mind to accept them without suspicion. I couldn't tell if anyone was waiting in the alley beneath but wasn't too much concerned. Listening would be as effective as watching from then on. A man doesn't climb five floors of metal rigging without sound.

I pawed my way back to the living room and pulled a shade aside to search the shadows of the street. There were trees. One of them—almost directly across from the mouth of the alley— bulked suggestively near the base. I studied it until my eyes wouldn't hold it any longer.

Then the bulge detached itself from the tree, and the person it had been walked purposefully down the street. It could be either a man or a woman; there was no sound of footsteps. With a person prepared to climb iron ladders quietly there would be no sound of footsteps on a sidewalk.

As I was trying to decide if he had seen my light or the movement of the shade and given it up for the night, a matter of several minutes, I was startled by the telephone. Lorry? I reached out in the dark, then changed my mind. It needn't be Lorry. She would call again, perhaps. Sometime later. The intruder, with plenty of time to get to a pay phone on the busy corner, would call once. Only once. It rang a dozen times before it gave up.

I went back to the kitchen to wait and listen.

My heart pumped off five minutes—ten. I rehearsed over and over in my mind how I would hear him on the fire escape, then make my way to a closet which opened off the long hall providing a peek at every other door in the apartment. The closet had the additional advantage of placing me where I could follow him from behind, whichever way he turned.

I sensed a movement outside and below and leaned farther toward the window, listening. A soft scraping and a dulled metallic note announced the end of rehearsal. The performance was on.

I retired to the closet, stood in the half-open door waiting for his entrance, and for him to settle down some place and start searching. The kitchen table creaked. Then there was a soft thud on the linoleum—undoubtedly a rubber sole. A waiting silence, then a series of small, cautious, padding sounds which cued the closing—to a crack—of my closet door. The erratic glances of a flashlight nipped at the crack, never directly, then stopped. In a moment I heard a drawer being pulled open. It would be the top drawer of the bureau. My visitor was systematic, taking up exactly where he had left off.

After a few moments the drawer was shoved shut. Almost immediately I heard gropings and scrapings so close to my head they seemed to be in the closet with me. The intruder was searching the bedroom closet, which was, apparently, back to back with mine. I found myself becoming impatient with him as he went over places I'd covered.

The light brushed my door again—close this time. Scuffing steps came into the hall, hesitated, and faded out toward the living room. A chair scraped; scraped again. I eased the door open far enough to get a look up the hall, then more as I saw the flashlight's glow showing steadily beyond. A half step out the door let me see him at the desk—a dark mass huddled forward—his back toward me. His arms moved as he shuffled papers around and held them toward the light. If he wanted anything in that mess other than the money which wasn't there, he'd be away from the desk in a hurry.

After ten minutes of controlling my breathing and my position, I knew it wasn't the money. After ten more I decided that it couldn't have been the envelope addressed to Trask either. He was reading all that junk I'd seen and stacking it carefully to one side.

I was cooking up ideas about facing the guy down when he started to put everything neatly back where he found it. It took a long time. The hallway was suffocatingly hot.

Finally the figure stood erect. As he closed the desk, I stepped back into my closet. I heard the squeak of a rubber sole, turned against hardwood. The pad of steps entered the hall. The guy was headed for the reducing room. He stopped exactly in front of my closet door. The light shone forward, not at the closet. Small comfort.

A faint odor, elusive yet familiar, drifted in to me. I was too busy being alert to place it. I was figuring what to do when the door was jerked open. I had a gun and a permit to carry it— back at my apartment.

The steps moved forward. I breathed again and heard a light switch snap somewhere beyond. A dim haze, washing the blackness the figure had left behind, told me the light wasn't in the hall. It had to be in one of the rooms behind. I hadn't heard the door open, which left out the reducing room and left in the bathroom and a spare bedroom, both of which I had looked over. I took a chance on pushing the door open a little and looking down the hall—the hard way because the door opened toward the living room. The light was in the bathroom. Unless nature, in its infinite vagary, had made sudden demands on the guy, bathroom searching had sinister implications. This might be the killer.

On the supposition that he'd turn the light off before he came back into the hall, I got head and shoulders out in order to hear better—a move which took me well out of the closet. I watched the lighted door for a shadow or a movement and listened.

The familiar odor taunted me, and I tried again to place it. The more I thought about it, the more intense it became;

seemed so close I wondered if it might have come from a garment hanging in my hiding place.

I remembered suddenly, in a blinding, pervading brilliance that left me with no thought except a determination to protect my face as I fell. My hands pushed against the floor—the right one remembered carpet. The runner in the hall. I was on my hands and knees, with a painful blaze of light above my head.

Some drops of blood had fallen on the back of my hand. I wiped it on my face. The odor came back, this time only in memory. I couldn't have smelled a steak frying.

It had been apple blossom—and applejack!

Sometime—a long time—later I'd climbed off the floor to find Eve Trask standing there.

"Get up, Doc!"

I didn't feel like chatting. Frankly, I didn't feel like getting up either.

"I said get up! Keep your hands in front of you!"

I got my head up, trying to avoid the direct glare of the flashlight. A pair of rubber-soled sport shoes, dark blue, like the slacks, a sleeve shoved forward, partly in the light . . .

"Don't make any quick moves. Just get on your feet."

It was Eve's voice—the tough one, the one that sounded like she had a gun in her hand.

This time she had!

13

Blood dribbled down my face and splattered on the back of my hand. Eve held the light steadily toward the floor, and I knew the gun was pointed, just as steadily, at my body. I raised my head a little and got a look at it projecting into the circle of brightness. It wasn't much of a gun—something like a twenty-five automatic—but I wanted it some place else. A small gun just makes a smaller hole.

"Get on your feet, Doc, then walk ahead. Follow the light." Somehow her voice wasn't nasty. What was it? Maybe it sounded tired. I got up.

"I don't know what you're doing here, Eve, but—"

"I'm certain you don't. Walk along and don't make any fast moves." She backed down the hall toward the living room and I tottered ahead. She made me stand away from her, switched on the lights, pocketed her flashlight, and stared at me. She was wearing a mannish hat of dark felt. After a while she said, "Sit down and keep your hands flat on the arms of the chair."

I sat down with an earnest resolution not to lose my high-priced dinner. Eve sat across from me, the little gun resting firmly on her thigh. She brushed her face with her free hand and spoke quietly.

"What were you looking for, Doc?"

"You."

She thought that over briefly. "By name? Were you looking for me or just anybody?"

"Just anybody—whoever broke in here last night—"

She gave this a sharp take, then another. "*Last* night? You're sure you don't mean *Friday* night?"

"Last night, Eve. Why try to kid me?"

The woman looked honestly puzzled. I began to believe her before she spoke. "I wish I were kidding you. Did someone break in here last night?"

"Yes. Through the kitchen window by the fire escape—at least that's the way he went out. Seem familiar?"

"Shut up!" She wasn't tired any more; stung it in. "This is important. Were you here?"

"No. Lorry came in and scared him off."

"Scared him off before— Had he taken anything?"

Had he—if there had been someone else? Not the five thousand, certainly. Maybe the envelope with Huck Trask's name on it. "Lorry didn't seem to think so."

Eve's lips tightened around her teeth. "She wouldn't have— *seemed* to think so." She got up and walked slowly toward me, her gun well in front of her. "Did Johnny Mallo have any money on him Friday night, in his wallet or hidden around?"

"Nobody said anything about it. What sort of money? How much?"

"A lot." She shook her head slowly. "She wouldn't have told you about any money either. Forget it."

"Is that what you were looking for?"

"No."

"Whose was it?"

She turned a pair of very hard eyes on me. "It was Johnny's. Shut up and forget it. Now we'll get you out of the picture—at least for a while. I've got things to do and I'm damned well going to do them without your interference."

"How about with my help, instead."

She frowned and shook her head again. "Go back to the bathroom and wash the blood off your face." A little vigorous motion of the gun. "Get going."

Eve stood in the doorway while I washed. The cold water helped a lot. I got an idea of throwing the towel in her face; gave it up in favor of no holes, even small ones, in my intestines.

She'd backed up to the door of the reducing room when I came
out into the hall again.

"Into the kitchen now!"

I trudged ahead of her and turned in at the kitchen door.
The flashlight followed me, down low. In the legs would be
better, but not good.

"Pick up that chair and come out. If you try to throw it at
me, I'll shoot you."

I got the chair and started forward. Eve backed slowly around
the corner toward the living room. "Now take it down to your
closet and sit on it!"

"Good Lord, Eve! I'd smother in the damned place! Just because you've learned how to breathe in that office of yours—"

"You're getting a break. Get in there and sit down and shut
up, then I'll tell you something."

I sat. My jailer leaned against the wall opposite the door.
"Listen, Doc, I suppose you mean well and all that, but you've
got your neck out. You've been interfering with things that are
not your business—even in your capacity as the common people's Ellery Queen. They're my business—mine and the Mallos'
and Huck's. Even your police friends know that."

I think her mouth quivered a little. I quivered all over. "My
police friends know that Johnny was murdered, if that interests
you. Talk about *my* neck being out—"

Common people's Ellery Queen, indeed! I damned near told
her they knew how he was killed too.

"That's a lot of defensive rot! You're touchy. You don't know
enough about our affairs to make police trouble—public trouble—for anybody. As it is, you've made private trouble for us
all." She lifted her arm and started to close the door.

"Wait a minute! You're a little highhanded about all this,
aren't you? How are you going to explain illegal entry and—"

"Illegal hooey! I've got a picture of you making a complaint
that I broke into a beautiful woman's apartment and found you.
Maybe you're looking for that sort of publicity. Katie Storm—"

"That's where you're mistaken." She knew perfectly well she
wasn't. "You can't laugh off that gun, Eve. Armed—"

She looked at me with that gleaming, toothy smile.

"What gun?"

She slammed the door and turned the key. I listened a few moments and heard her banging around in the reducing room. I wasn't seriously concerned about smothering, but the damned closet was hot enough to provide an unpleasant reminder of Johnny's cabinet.

After a time I heard the kitchen table squeak, and I set about the business of stamping on the floor. At first I was satisfied just to tramp around, but nothing happened, and I got madder and madder. By the time I had been through Kipling's *Boots* a couple of times and was well into a ballet version of Vachel Lindsay's *Congo,* there was a tremendous pounding on the outer door. After some delay and shouting, the closet door opened and the manager stood back as if he were expecting an explosion.

"What in the world?"

"I got myself locked in—"

"But that's impossible!" He peered at me. "Doctor! Your head! You've been struck!"

"It was just a friendly romp. I've got to look around here some more. Thanks for—liberating me. Now, if you'll be good enough to—"

That really got his feathers up. "I'll not accept a joking explanation of this, Dr. Connor. No one, to my knowledge, has entered this apartment—legitimately, at least—since you arrived. I have been"—the little guy pouted his breast—"watching."

"I'm sure you have, mister—I don't think you told me your name."

"Banton. Howard J. Banton."

I resisted Bantam. "Mr. Banton. I'm afraid I was joking because I was confronted by a very delicate and embarrassing situation—a personal trust I had undertaken for Mr. Mallo. It concerns—"

Banton put his hand to his lips and said, "Sshh! I have been very obtuse. I think I know whom it concerned."

Then Mickey Mallo walked into the hall from the living room. He looked angrily at me. "What are you doing here, Doc?"

"Waiting for you, Mick."

The boy was puzzled and suspicious. Banton cut in. "My apologies, Doctor. I see it very clearly now." He turned to young Mallo. Snapped his beak. "I have no doubt, Mallo, that the injuries—er—sustained by Dr. Connor were intended for you." Back to me. "In view of the extreme delicacy of the situation, I shall—forget it. You are quite certain there will be no further disturbance?"

I hastened to assure him. "None whatever, Mr. Banton. Mickey and I will leave, almost at once. We have a few things to arrange first. Thank you for your help—and your unusual understanding."

He bowed and stomped off. He knew perfectly well he'd make his building look like a bawdy house if he'd yelled for the police. The old crow!

As Banton's heels died down the hall, Mickey said, "What right have you got in here?"

"Sit down, Mick. I'll tell you. I wasn't kidding when I told the manager we had some arrangements to make."

The boy eased himself into a chair and kept alert eyes on me. I sat opposite him. "Your sister-in-law asked me to come here. Somebody broke into the apartment last night and she was frightened. Somebody broke in again tonight."

He was startled. "*Tonight?* Is that how you got socked on the head?"

"Exactly." The kid squirmed. "What would you know about that, Mick?"

"Why would I know anything about it?" Surly.

"I don't think you do know too much about it. If you did, you'd get rid of that envelope of Huck Trask's and run like hell. He's a tough baby when he wants to be."

Young Mallo was thoroughly frightened. "Huck is a friend of mine."

"Was."

"He—I—I'm trying to help him. What do you mean—was?"

"Have you given Trask the envelope—the one with his name on it?" He stared at the floor and said nothing. "You found it here last night, didn't you, Mallo?"

"What's it to you if I did? You sure got a nerve when it comes to other people's business."

"It's public business now—the sort of public business that you can't shut up, Mickey. Maybe it started out as a reasonably harmless family row—counting the Trasks and Ralph Pack as family—"

He looked up quickly. "Why Ralph Pack?"

"Leave him out if you want, for the moment. It could have been a harmless—if very unpleasant—row except for one thing. One of the five people concerned killed your brother."

"Are you still kidding yourself about that?"

"No. Not any more. *You're* kidding *your*self about it. Johnny was murdered."

"The police—"

"The police will be pounding on your tail within twenty-four hours, kid. As it stands you don't look too good."

"Listen! I'm not standing still for that kind of shoving around. I know that Johnny wasn't murdered. Dr. Pack told—"

"Wait a minute. I know what Pack told Lorry. It doesn't mean a thing. Your brother was murdered, and one of the five of you did it." I watched some of the conviction, or confidence, go out of him. Wondered, too, if he'd been cautioned about sleeping pills and sweat baths at some time or other. "You're not helping yourself any by trying to steal five thousand dollars of his."

Mickey put his hands on the arms of his chair, started to rise, sank back. "What—five thousand dollars?"

"The money that everybody seems to want except the person it belongs to. Lorry doesn't know it exists; but the rest of you are taking turns searching for it. Where did it come from, kid? I think you'd better tell me. You're in a hell of a personal jam."

"I didn't kill Johnny, Doc." It came out with a surprising gentleness.

"I don't think you did. If I thought so I wouldn't be asking you to tell me the truth—you wouldn't. Where did the money come from? Did your brother have it with him Friday night?"

"Yes. Huck Trask paid it to him."

"For what?"

Mickey sat very still, said nothing, but shook his head slowly. He clenched and opened his fists; rubbed his hands on his trouser leg. He got up and walked across the room; picked up his hat. I went over to him and took hold of his arm. "Would you rather tell me—or the cops?"

I let him pull his arm away. He stood away from me for a moment; stared at the desk. "Do you know where the money is, Doc?"

"Yes."

"Is it—safe? I mean has anybody got it that—shouldn't have it?"

"No. It's safe enough. Who did you think might have got it?"

"Why—" He put his hat on and leaned back against the table. "Trask?"

"Yes."

"And you were trying to protect it—for Lorry?"

"Yes. She didn't know Johnny had it or what it was for. I was afraid Johnny might have given it away before he— Friday night."

"To whom, Mick?"

He pushed a rug around with his foot a few times before he spoke. "You said it could have been a family row, Doc—just that and nothing more. Then you said that somebody killed my brother."

"Somebody did."

He spoke slowly. Thoughtfully. "Before, when I didn't think it was possible anybody could have murdered Johnny, I wouldn't have said anything so as not to hurt some people's feelings. If what you say is true, I— Hell, Doc! I could make an awful mistake. I've got to be sure. There's just one thing I've got to find out. Just one thing, then maybe I'll tell you a lot of things."

"All right, Mick." I got a brain storm. "How would you like to give Lorry the money yourself? Big-brother stuff."

He looked wistful as hell. Apparently he and Pack belonged to the same fan club. "Gee, Doc—"

"Let's go get it." Mickey followed me back to the reducing room and I pulled the envelope off the drawer and handed it to him. Good old Doc! Juvenile delinquency cured at all hours! As we walked back to the living room I stuck a straw in my cake. "Where did it come from, Mick?"

It came out pretty doughy. The boy gave me a disappointed look and handed me the envelope. "You give it to her, Doc. I've got to be sure. I told you that. Besides, I don't think I want to carry that much around." He turned away and started for the door.

"All right. Maybe it's better this way. I'll hold the money until you feel ready to help me straighten this mess out, then you can turn it over to Lorry. O.K.?"

"Yeah. That'll be all right."

"Now what about Huck Trask's envelope?"

"That's one of the things I can't talk about—yet. I admit I've got it. I think I had a right to get it."

"But it belongs to Trask?"

"I—guess so—now."

"What do you mean—now?"

He indicated the envelope in my hand. "Now I know he hasn't got that." The boy walked to the door. "I've got nothing more to say, Doc. Not tonight, anyway."

"That's all right with me, only don't hold off too long. I know you don't want to hurt anyone, but let's be sure someone doesn't hurt you. O.K.?"

"Sure, Doc. O.K."

I sent the boy on his way and did a little straightening up; took the canned goods off the window sills; put the drawer back in the rubbing table, carefully reattaching the empty envelope. I closed and locked the kitchen window and went home.

I took a shower, put on a comfortable terry-cloth robe, and mixed a modest drink. Young Mallo had the Trask envelope. No doubt about that. It probably hadn't contained money. Or had it? And had the money found its way to the rubbing table? Five thousand dollars seemed plenty to encompass any deal Johnny could have made with the people concerned. Yet Eve Trask had been reading the papers she had examined, rather than roughing through them for the substantial feel of five new bills.

One thing I had neglected. If Huck Trask had been involved in the Nautilus deal—and I felt that he must have been—there would have been some pretty heavy betting on the horse around the country. The price on Agency Man suggested that little of the Nautilus money had got back to the track, which means careful planning and timing. I made up my mind to do a little investigating in the morning. That sort of thing gets around.

My office files were the only things in the place that would lock securely, and I went through to put away the money. There was a current of air on my face as I opened the office, though I'd left the window closed. I snapped on the lights. The hall door was standing open and the desk was a shambles. It had been thoroughly searched—thoroughly, hurriedly, and carelessly. The cigar box still contained its thirty or forty dollars. If robbery was the motive, it hadn't been petty.

I locked the outside door again and went back to the living room. My small desk showed signs of having been disturbed. My visitor had been in my living quarters. And then I thought of Sauki-no-no, called her; looked in every room and closet. No cat. My sore head pounded a terrible accompaniment to a terrible thought. Sauki-no-no was gone!

I gathered my robe around me and rushed out into the night!

14

The months which pass between the first crushing impact of such a disaster and its final recounting—frozen into the book which you have in your hand—seem hardly time enough to implant, in the rich tradition of Broadway, a new and eerie folk tale.

Yet the people are heard, these evenings, to speak in hushed tones concerning the nocturnal appearance of a mad monk in the public ways—white-robed and filled with strange mutterings and callings. It is told that he walked in sandals bound by a primitive thong to his bare feet, that he shunned passers-by, and materialized only briefly in the lighted places.

But in the dark passages—the narrow, littered areas where honest men dared not venture and only the drunk lay fearless—the mad monk was heard to call on his exotic gods.

"Sauki—Sauki—Sauki-no-noooooo—"

Morning brought no relief from my desolation. Katie would never forgive me. Sauki-no-no had been her constant companion—the devoted sharer of such home life as a busy unmarried woman could create in the frigid atmosphere of Beekman Place. Hell! Katie might even look for *other* companionship!

I tried to cheer myself by repeating the old saying that cats come back. No good. This was no coming-back kind of cat—this purebred Siamese, raised from kittenhood in a formal East Side section where nobody would think of asking for a frozen fish. Even if she did come back, the social implications were— unthinkable! I tried desperately to remember more about my

soiled gray friend of the alley. I had always taken it for granted
he was a tom.

I phoned advertisements to every lost-and-found column in
town before I started a dispirited search for evidence of a betting coup on Nautilus. I called Elegant Johnson.

"How would you like to do a little job for me?"

"I dunno, Doc. With or without fisticuffs?"

"None with me, at least, Elegant. I want you to snoop down
some betting information."

"With this face, nobody would give me anything. What kind
of betting information?"

I explained. He listened carefully, suggested a couple of
likely sources. Then, "Look here, Doc, you said this was a
homicide. I don't like it too much. What about Eddie Marsh?"

"No trouble with Marsh, Elegant; he'll be busy for days asking people pleasant, orderly questions."

"I take it that you want to ask unpleasant, disorderly questions?"

"Maybe. I can't tell yet. What about it?"

"I smell a very strong odor, but I need the dough—twenty
bucks a day and expenses."

"If you get beaten up I'll treat you. Free. See you—when?"

He promised to get right after the people mentioned and
report back.

While I was getting ready to go out, Lorry called, all very
sweet and co-operative. She could be reached any time at Virginia 9-6717 and what had happened last night? Without knowing exactly why, I told her that nothing had happened, that I'd
simply waited around awhile and gone home. She seemed satisfied with that, and I made a note to call Howard J. Banton and
romance him into secrecy. Before I hung up, I asked her if she
knew any reason why Huck Trask might pay Johnny a substantial sum of money. She gave it quite a lot of thought.

"I haven't any idea at all, Doc. I've told you how bitter they
were toward each other. Johnny's never missed a chance to show
it. Do you think Huck might have owed him money?"

"I don't know. Maybe it wasn't Trask, but I think somebody did."

"Why?"

"From the appearance of things. I'll tell you about that later. How about Mickey, Lorry? How did he speak of the Trasks? Privately, I mean."

"At first he used to scoff about some hustler acting as his agent. Lately, though, they've been as thick as thieves."

On this suggestive note I signed off, got my hat, and ventured out into a steaming morning to call on a guy called Dolly Browning. Dolly was something of a figure among the boys who conduct one of our largest national industries—off-track betting. The single word *Investments* on the door to his large, modestly furnished offices covered a multitude of parlays, although he probably hadn't actually booked a bet in years. It was reported, gossipwise, that he owned a major clearinghouse for an imposing percentage of the town's thousands of bookmakers.

I sat opposite him—a small man who moved quickly with his hands; slowly and carefully with his head. He was cordial.

"It's good to see you, Doc. What've you got on your mind?"

"I'm trying to keep a small friend out of trouble."

Browning smiled. "That's worthy of you. Who's your small friend?"

"Mickey Mallo. I think he's outsmarted himself."

"His brother couldn't have been too smart. What's the boy done?"

"He made a bad bet the other day, Dolly. Against himself. I'm wondering how many others he might have taken along with him."

The man across the desk frowned; picked up his phone. "I may be able to tell you something about that." He asked his secretary to bring in the letter to Alan Copey. "If I'm not mistaken, I've just dictated a note on the subject."

The girl brought in a carbon copy of a typed letter to which was attached a handwritten one, apparently received. She said, "The original is in the mail, Mr. Browning."

"This will do, thank you." When the door had closed behind the girl, Dolly said, "This letter came yesterday. It's from Alan Copey, the band leader. He's a pleasant enough guy, but an intemperate horse player." He handed me the note.

> Dear Dolly,
> Salutations. I've been a chump again and have been bad. It's only four hundred bucks but it made me sore. With my messenger copy of *Huck's Hot Horses* (it comes every evening) there was an enclosure—a typed note. It said to call Columbus 8-4457 if I wanted in on a terrific deal the next day (Friday). I called, and a man told me Trask absolutely refused to appear in the picture, but had run onto a fix—that if I'd bet two hundred for each of us, he'd give me the horse over the phone. It was a thing called Nautilus in the fourth. He instructed me to send his slip, made out to "Mr. O.K.", to Apartment 6-B, The Venturia. I did. Of course the favorite won and I lost my dough. Did you hear anything about it? I thought I wouldn't face Trask down with it until I had him to rights.
> Sincerely,
>
> Alan

It was my problem child, all right. I looked up at Dolly Browning. "I wonder how many were sent out."

"Probably quite a big list. It isn't like Trask, though. He's always had a policy against giving out single horses. The messenger service is the same as the track card with the exception of editing for scratches, of course—just an extra edition for the telephone betters. Do you suppose the boy rigged it up himself?"

"He could have. The address is right, and he has access, I suppose, to anything in Trask's office. They were very friendly."

"He could have stuffed the notes in some of the mailings with the pretense of helping Trask possibly." Browning smiled gently. "Still crusading for racing, eh, Doc?"

I hadn't thought of it that way. "I suppose so. It's a big part of my life, Dolly. I love the sport and most of the people who have any standing in it."

"And the rest?"

"You know what I think—I hate chiselers and grifters, the sort who make anybody else look bad by being in the same city block. They make a highly profitable business of teaching the public to suspect race-track manipulation so their worthless tips will seem more credible." I caught myself waving my arms—a demonstration which inevitably accompanies my tirades on the subject. "Hell, Dolly—you know—"

"Of course I know, Doc. I've been around a long time; have watched it build up to the point where the racing associations have had to resort to police systems to protect themselves—not nearly so much against corruption within racing as to discredit influences from the outside. This letter is a typical example."

"Sure. To Alan Copey it's simply a crooked deal—one of many—that didn't come off. I'm surprised he'd have the guts to admit he had any part of it."

"His willingness to admit it to me is pretty unflattering. He takes it for granted that my—fraternity—has slipped up. Fortunately the bookmaker doesn't have to corrupt either betters or jockeys. The Copeys are that way already, and the tipsters and sure-thing boys, unhappily, get to an occasional kid rider, because he was galloping horses when he should have been playing ball at school."

"So the bookmakers corrupt the politicians."

Browning didn't laugh. "It stinks. It used to take brains to make book. You had to know the horses and the conditions. Now all you've got to know is a soft cop."

"And a few people like Alan Copey."

"That's right. People like Copey are convinced that racing is dishonest and sneer to their friends about it. But offer to let them in on a supposed fix and they pant like a hound." Dolly threw the letter into his outgoing tray. "Of course they can't squawk when they lose. It's an old gag."

"Is that what you wrote Copey?"

"Exactly. In Anglo-Saxon. Want to read it?"

"No." I got ready to go. I felt rotten about Mickey, whether Trask was in it or not. My impulsive and sentimental gesture of the night before seemed as silly as it probably was. "In case anything can be done to straighten the kid out—"

Browning stood up and put out his hand. "Forget it, Doc. I won't have anything to say. I'm afraid the nest is pretty badly fouled as it is."

Coming uptown again, I wondered where I should go from there. Whoever had searched my rooms—Trask, Lorry Mallo, Mickey, who?—must have been after either the money or Trask's envelope. If it was the envelope, I could leave out Mick—he had it. Lorry's invitation could have been a neat booby trap, except that somebody had actually broken into her place.

When I got home, Elegant Johnson was waiting for me in my living room. He stood up and grinned as I came in. "I hope you don't mind, Doc. I thought it was just as well if I wasn't seen hanging around outside."

"It's O.K., Elegant. How did you get in?"

He produced a celluloid card from his pocket. "Your lock is leaky."

"Did you learn anything?"

Johnson frowned; scratched his head. "Yeah—I think so. I don't exactly know what to do with it yet."

"Maybe I do. Sit down and tell me."

He stretched his lean frame over a chair. "First I went around two, three places to see if I could find some heavy play on the Nautilus horse. I got nothing. No really big bets, no new faces, no gossip—at least that's what they told me. Sometimes they don't talk too much about that kind of thing."

"No. It could fit. I don't think it was much of a transaction. Then what?"

"Then I went up to see Sam Fenner. I figured he wouldn't have hired me in the first place unless he knew quite a lot about what he was doing. A guy that tightropes around the edges of the law like he does has got to be sure."

"That sort doesn't talk, either, Elegant."

"Sam talked some. I threw a scare into him."

"How?"

"Hell! I told him what I thought of him for sending me out on a case without telling me I was getting mixed up in a homicide. He howled, and said it was a simple surveillance and where did I get the idea it was a killing. I told him you were working on the thing with Marsh, and that Marsh would be sore. I demanded to know who had him hire me—"

"Did he tell you?"

Elegant turned to me with a broad grin on his homely mug. "No. He was very cagey about it. He got red in the face and sputtered at me; said, 'I'll have you know my client is one of the city's most highly respected—er—oomph—professional men!'"

"Well, how do you do! The good doctor gets around, doesn't he!"

"Getting your money's worth so far, Doc?"

"Handsomely! Don't tell me there's more."

"There's a tidbit, boss—just a tidbit." He put the edge of the chair in the middle of his back and stared at the ceiling. "I gained it in a venture that was—shall we say—somewhat beyond the call of duty."

"Is this bribery, Johnson?"

"Of the pleasanter sort—say just a ration of your very choice bourbon—"

I hauled out the Forester and set him up in business. After some lip smacking and other oriental symbols of appreciation he said, "I made a fast visit to the Trask office, which seemed to be unoccupied at the moment because the tenants were having breakfast downstairs, and gave the customer list a little attention."

"You broke in?"

"That, my friend, is against the law. On finding the door locked, I attempted to leave my card, the most convenient place being the crack between—"

"All right. I see. What about the list?"

"There seemed to be three. A big one was labeled *General*. Then there was a smaller one marked *Messenger Service*. I passed

them both up for one they'd tabbed *Messenger Service, Special.*"
Elegant took a long, slow drink. "It was most illuminating."

"What do you want me to do? Guess?"

"Not at all. While the list was hardly of Social Register caliber, it *was* distinguished by the inclusion of—and I quote—'one of the city's most highly respected—er—oomph—professional men.'"

"Pack!"

The goon beamed happily. "You *did* guess it, didn't you!"

I was still guessing some twelve hours later when I went to bed.

15

At five-twenty my alarm clock started jumping up and down on the night stand. It had been set for half an hour later, but that's what you get for letting them stand too long in the barn.

I got some comfortable clothing on, pinned a note to the office door saying nine-thirty, and headed for the Eighth Avenue subway. If any outsider would know about the old Mallo-Trask relationships, Frank Latch might. He had contracts on both boys from their early apprenticeships—a matter which involves considerably more than riding instruction.

Eddie Marsh's orderly questions would lead him to Huck Trask almost at once, and I had to have something to offer the big cop before he started throwing punches at me. The conviction that Johnny Mallo's murder was hatched back there in Florida wouldn't leave me, even in the face of such current complications as the Nautilus deal. Eve's "so much from a long time back. Stuff that should have stayed back there and wouldn't" keyed my thinking. From the subway, a bus hauled me to the back side of the track where a short cut through a little patch of woods and a Chinese vegetable garden leads to Mr. Fitz's barns. I hollered hi to some of the old familiars and saw, as always, a couple of new faces. They should have a meeting of the Mr. Fitz alumni association sometime—it includes many a master horseman.

As I passed the office I didn't bother to look in. At that hour John Aloysius would have been breakfasting cozily at Sheepshead Bay. He starts worrying at precisely 8 a.m.

Frank Latch was standing moodily by the corner of his shed, pawing at a handful of timothy. I said, "It's not bad with a little cream and sugar, Frank."

He looked up. Smiled. "Doc, take a look at that hay." He shoved the wad at me. "A horse'd just as soon eat an old mule-skin mitten."

It was pretty bad—burned up in the field and poorly headed. "The trouble with you Hackensack horsemen is that you try to do it like your grandfathers did. There hasn't been any good timothy hay since White Favor kicked the door off the tack room."

"So what do I feed—Post Toasties?"

"Alfalfa."

"I'm scared of it." Latch turned away from me and shouted down the line. "He goes with the first set, Paddy. Put his boots on and be sure they're clean inside." He looked back at me curiously. "What're you doing up at this hour, Doc?"

"I came out to ask you a couple of questions about Johnny Mallo."

"About John?"

"He came to me the day before he died and suggested he might have run into some—unpleasantness. I was to talk it over with him the next day—" I let it hang.

Frank spoke deliberately, carefully. "Did Johnny tell you what the unpleasantness was about?"

"It had to do with Mickey—and the Trasks."

He stood thoughtfully a moment, then went down the shed to his foreman; spoke to him for several minutes. When he came back, he said, "Let's go over to the kitchen and have some coffee, Doc. I think we've got some things to discuss."

The early crowd was gone and the late crew hadn't come in. We sat in a corner booth and called for coffee and crullers. Latch stirred sugar into his cup, tasted the coffee, and leaned back.

"Doc, I've spent a lot of years minding my own business, but that don't keep me from knowing some of the things that are going on around me. You can't spend seven, eight years with

a couple of youngsters without getting some ideas about them.
I've had a few ideas about the Mallo boys."

He drank some of his coffee and lit a cigarette. "Each of the
two has always had a hole in him—a fault that seemed to get
worse as time went on. The older brother was deathly scared
of poverty. He was a hard lad with a dollar, John was—scrimp-
ing, saving, writing sums on pieces of paper all the time. He
hounded Mick until hell wouldn't have it, even when the boy
was in the ice-cream-cone stage. He made Mick pay insurance
premiums so big they kept him broke even for normal spending
money. It's not that I'm against a rider saving his money—"

"You say Johnny was always like that—since you knew him?"

"Pretty much so. I suspect that Lorry is part and parcel of
the same breed. After they got married, John was worse."

"Speaking of Lorry, how much do you know about Johnny's
bust-up with Eve Trask in Florida?"

"What I know and what I suspect are two different things,
Doc. John was a serious, ambitious country kid, and the Corcoran girl was town-smart. The boy met her through Trask—"

"Did Trask and Johnny get along at that time?"

"David and Jonathan. Trask had been handling some riders
but had lost 'em because he was lazy. John used to try to get me
to agree to let Trask take over his book. Then, one day—and I'd
forgotten about it until some months later—John started col-
lecting all the tout cards he could get his hands on. He'd bring
'em back to the barn, compare each one with the results, and
then put it away in the tack room—all marked with profit and
loss. When I asked him if he was thinking of making a career of
horse playing, he asked me a lot of questions about how much
these fellers made out of a sheet like that. As I say, I forgot
about it when he seemed to lose interest. I didn't think of it
again until *Huck's Hot Horses* come out the following spring in
New York."

Just like that! I wanted to yell, but didn't interrupt.

"Well, to go back to Miami, sometime after the tout-card
craze, John went into a slump. He rode like an old woman and

grouched around the barn until I worried the reason out of him. It seems that Eve Corcoran had played him for a sucker."

"Doing a bit of hustling for Trask?"

"That's right. John didn't say anything about any business dealings with Trask, but it looked like Eve had wheedled him into something, and when John got serious about marrying her, she run off and hid."

"So Johnny married the hotel switchboard operator on the rebound!"

"It looked that way. I never had anything against Lorry, except maybe that she was looking for a soft berth and that she might have learned where she could find one on her switch-board—listening in."

"Could be." Now she was set for a benefit or a hundred and fifty thousand dollars! "I guess Johnny's beautiful friendship with Trask didn't live through that."

"Not any. I don't suppose they've had a dozen words since. Not in public, anyway. The boy hated Trask's guts."

"Although they might have had a business deal going all that time—until now."

"I've thought so, but I've never said anything about it." Latch stood up. I dropped a half dollar on the table and we walked outside. "That make any sense for you, Doc?"

"It makes very important sense, Frank. It—puts people where they belong in the picture."

Latch frowned; plodded along toward the barn. Finally he said, "You been associated with so much police business—I guess you'd understand my feeling—" He was having a rough trip.

"I think Johnny was murdered. He could have been, despite what you read in the papers."

"If he could've been, he probably was—as much as I hate to say it." He walked on in silence for a while. "I'm letting Mickey go, Doc."

"Have you told him?"

"He's been galloping horses for me last couple of mornings. I'm telling him this morning."

"Just why are you turning him loose?"

"Let's call it brawling in the jock house and general—unruliness, shall we, Doc? The boy would be better off away from the horses."

"He'd be better off away from something or somebody. That's sure." As we approached the barn I said, "Frank, you could help the kid a lot by making a—sort of a bargain with him."

He looked a little surprised. "Bargain? What sort of a bargain?"

"Let him go on galloping horses for you in the mornings on the terms that he accepts no more race mounts. I have a reason for asking. Will you do that?"

"How can I? The boy will be arrested for killing his brother—"

"I think not. I'm interested in seeing that he doesn't get arrested for something else. Keep him out of trouble for a time, will you, Frank? I don't know why I've appointed myself defender of such a mean little heel, but, for some reason, I have."

"Well, hell! If you think you can get anywhere with the kid I'll go along. Shall I tell him you put in a word for him?"

"It might be a good thought."

As I left Latch and started for the Rockaway gate, Mickey rode the big Ashford colt out from under the shed. He was abnormally busy knotting his reins and didn't look up. The kid that got tired of no ice-cream cones and tried to turn a fast buck! Johnny could have made the boy's life pretty miserable. That would go for any of them, of course.

I flagged a cab and made the subway just in time for the morning rush. A couple of well-upholstered standees surrounded me and I went on thinking of what Mallo could have done to people.

Trask, for instance. The man is broke, in love with a very fancy gal, and limited in business experience to the race track. His pal, the very successful young jockey, has dough all over the place. Trask sells Mallo the idea of bank rolling a selection card—with pleasant nudges from the girl friend. Johnny goes for—what? Five grand? Everything is dandy, so maybe Trask signs a demand note.

Then everything gets not dandy any more. Little Mr. Moneybags goes for the big, beautiful blonde, and the b.,b.b. runs to Papa—marries him. The happy couple honeymoons at Jamaica (L.I.) trying to get out from under a note that is always due. Moneybags draws a substantial share of the gross weekly receipts and tweaks the Trask nose whenever anybody gets funny. So Huck finally digs up enough money, Johnny gets it—and gets dead the same night.

Of course there's one ironical twist that could have kept the thing going—and it was full of mean little impasses. Any time Trask decided to chuck it, go out of business, and tell Mallo to sue or whistle for his dough, Johnny would probably go out of business too. The old gentlemen with the white mustachios don't take kindly to working jockeys who publish tip sheets. Dispassionate selection of chances is hardly an avocation for a lad who's supposed to be up there whoopin' and hollerin'!

Lorry, too, may have felt the pinch. She possibly was, as Latch had suggested, something of a money counter herself, but you can get awfully tired of that sort of thing in a few years. The handsome and professionally sympathetic Pack would understand. Fourth-of-July flags stir no hearts when they're stored in bank vaults.

All that dough—and a top rider during his few best seasons puts away a package, even with the Federal takeout—all that dough sunk in insurance that probably wouldn't pay off! Irony again.

I got shoved off at Fifty-fourth Street and rode up the escalator with a high resolve to strike while the irony was hot.

16

I waded through the clinic without much enthusiasm and with quite a lot on my mind beside Rink Donnelly's stomach—a massive organ which had received and disposed of a considerable fortune in rich food and drink before it revolted from hot dogs and bad whisky.

It was crowding two when I finally got around to planning how to smoke somebody out on the Mallo-Trask relationship. I called Mickey on the theory he'd be home from the track. No answer. Then I called the Trask apartment and office. No answer. I couldn't locate Lorry Mallo. Maybe they'd all gone to the races together. Nice party!

At three-ten—I checked it—the telephone rang and Elegant Johnson came in simultaneously. I let Johnson in and picked up the phone, hoping for an answer to my lost and found.

"Doc—" It was Eve. Bad wire—like a country line.

"Hi. What's on your mind?"

"Have you seen Huck?"

"No." Midafternoon. "Isn't he at the track?"

"No. I'm at the track—at least across the street from the gate. They wouldn't let me phone from—"

"Did he get the sheet out?"

"It was delivered here, but he didn't turn up. The crew boss called me and I came out. I'm worried stiff." Her voice was tight, controlled.

"When did you hear from him last?"

"This morning when he left for the office. I went out shopping after that and didn't get back until around noon. The card should have been distributed by that time. That's when they called me."

"Did you call the office?"

"Yes, and so did the crew boss. There wasn't anybody there."

"How come you weren't at the office this morning?"

"I don't always go, and I had things to do."

"All right, Eve. Look; maybe you'd better stick at the track and I'll make some inquiries. If Huck turns up—as I expect he will—call here. There'll be somebody to answer. Meantime, I'll have a look around. You say you haven't been in the office this morning?"

"No. I called, you see, and—"

"That's all right. Phone the building so I can get a key, and I'll see if he's left a note or anything. He might have tried to call you."

Eve didn't seem much relieved. She sounded thoroughly shaken. "Doc! Something terrible's happened—I know it!"

"Don't be silly. What makes you think something terrible's happened?"

She didn't answer, so I went on. It wouldn't hurt, and it might set her up to do some talking later. She had plenty to do. "Listen, Eve; if anything terrible has happened, you'd better do a little explaining to me. As it is, I'm finding things out the hard way—the slow way."

"But what could I explain?" I had the feeling she'd stopped worrying about Trask and started doing a little side-stepping for herself.

"You could explain why you didn't tell me Johnny and Huck were in a deal together for one thing—a rather unpleasant one."

"I think it's pretty obvious why I didn't. Who told you?"

"Forget it. We can talk later. Stick close to the secretary's office. If I get anything, I'll call you there."

I left it that way and went back to Elegant. I didn't bother to explain to him—just told him I was expecting some calls and

to wait. In a misguided burst of hospitality I added that there
was a drink in the kitchen cabinet.

Before I left I tried the Trask office again. No answer.

The building management let me have a key and made me
sign for it. I went upstairs. There was no note on the door, but
the lights were burning inside. I passed through Eve's cubicle
to the office, then I went back to Eve's desk, picked up the telephone by the cord, and called Eddie Marsh—yelled at him to
get an ambulance and himself here right now.

Trask was on the floor beside his chair. He was living—just.
His pulse and respiration were bad. The left side of his head
was ripped open, and he had a mass of blood soaking, partly
congealed, through his white shirt at the right shoulder. They
were bullet wounds.

I cursed myself for not being able to do anything beyond
making sure there was no active external hemorrhage, and
looked around for the gun. By the time I couldn't find any,
people began to arrive—a radio-car man, an ambulance crew,
Eddie, and his first team—most of whom I knew.

A very competent-looking young man dumped his tools
down beside Trask, shoved me aside, and went to work. They
had him on the stretcher and off to the ambulance and oxygen
before Marsh and I had much chance to talk.

We walked over to the window. Eddie said, "Tell me about
it, Doc."

I told him what Eve had told me. His eyes roamed the room,
fastening on this and that for a moment, then going on to
something else. Phil Stoker, the print man, was digging around
with his properties which reminded me that Elegant Johnson's
would probably turn up on the filing cabinet. Eddie said, "Get
everything in both rooms, Phil; we'll have them all—or can get
'em." He turned to me. "Will Trask live, Doc?"

"He's alive. I'm a physician, not a soothsayer."

The big cop glanced at my face. "Your guess is better than
mine. What are you sore about?"

I didn't realize I was angry until he spoke. "I'm sorry. I'm
sore because I should have seen how to prevent this."

"How could you have prevented it?"

"Hell! I don't know—it has to be one of them. Nobody came in and shot Trask because he missed calling the third race."

"Wasn't he in on some sort of a sucker deal?"

"I don't think he knew anything about it. People might have thought he was in on it. It would amount to the same thing." It was silly. Nobody was going to shoot the guy because of a supposed race fix, unless it was for the kind of money that was, apparently, not involved in this one. It would have been all over town by Saturday. "I think Trask knew who killed Johnny."

Eddie said that could be. He walked casually over to the corner of the room and studied the wall. "Enders!"

One of the men came over. "Yes, sir?" The "sir" was for my benefit.

"Here's one. Get it out carefully."

Enders went back to his kit, and Marsh said, "Here's a miss or a ricochet, Doc." I went over and looked at it—a dull spot embedded in the plaster. Enders removed a neat patch of wall and came up with the slug.

"It's beat up pretty good, Lieutenant."

Eddie said, "There'll be at least one good one—the one in the shoulder, I should say. How about it, Doc?"

"I couldn't tell much when I saw it. Maybe."

Enders produced some cotton and a glassine envelope. "Light gun—like a twenty-five."

I hadn't thought of that. It hit me fast and hard. Coincidence that would account for it simply wouldn't be acceptable. I had looked down the barrel of that dirty little automatic in Johnny Mallo's apartment.

Eve Trask was sure something terrible had happened, was she? It made wonderfully good sense at the moment. Eddie followed Enders across the room and gave me time to think. I decided to forget the caliber of the slug until later. Eddie was moving too rapidly, right now, for any long explanations about a friendly armed robbery. This one would be long, indeed.

I told Marsh I thought I'd better call Eve, and went down to the lobby. She was waiting at the secretary's office.

"Doc! Have you heard anything?"

"Huck's been hurt, Eve"—I felt phony as a wig—"shot."

"Oh, dear God! How? *Doc!*—how is he?" I don't remember how she said it. I tried afterward to make sure my own hard disbelief hadn't warped it.

"He's badly injured. They've taken him to the hospital. I'd suggest you come to—"

"Which hospital? I've got to get to him. Where is he?"

Get to him? Brother!

I told her she wouldn't be able to see him and to hurry to my place as fast as she could get a cab from the track. I went upstairs again, kicking myself for thinking I could play cute games with women who climbed fire escapes with guns in their hands and hit people over the head with—whatever she'd hit me with. Eddie would be rough.

When I got back to the office he said, "There's a hell of a lot of procedure to go through here, Doc. Between this place and the precinct there are two, three hours. You be free after that?"

"Of course. At my apartment?"

"If you'd like. Sure, that'll be fine." He grinned. "I'll see you then, eh?"

"In other words—blow?"

"Blow. In another ten minutes we'll have visitors who've, in the past, been—somewhat critical of our association. I've managed to get myself back into reasonably good standing—"

"O.K., O.K., don't get upset—I'm on my way. Anybody special?"

"Very. Koch, no less."

"Give the big—solicitor—my love. I'll lay you six, two, and even he'll smell me around here after I've been gone an hour."

"He's already smelled you. He's tied it up with a couple of talks we had about Mallo. Let's not make another of those things out of this, Doc. You can't blame the guy."

"I don't blame him. Sometimes I don't like myself too well either. See you later."

I beat it with a sudden and disturbing addition to my memories—Elegant Johnson's one-man raid on Trask's office. I had thought of his prints on the file as something of a gag—before I found I'd probably been shielding a murderess.

When I got back I found that Johnson had made himself very much at home indeed. He sprawled, longer and looser than ever, in my big chair with my Forester bottle parked close at hand—about two bucks' worth off the top. He had his shoes off.

As I started to deliver the message to Garcia, he smiled gently and said, "Doc, I take it you lose some cats."

"Yes! A cat! Did somebody call?"

He piled himself, section by section, onto his feet. "Practically everybody called. They all got your cat."

"Hell, Elegant! They couldn't mistake her—black face, blue eyes, fawn body—"

"Long, ratty tail?"

"*Whip* tail. That's right. Did somebody describe her?"

"Yeah. *You* did. That's the cat I seen foolin' around the alley when I come in. Damndest-lookin' cat I ever seen! Why, say—"

I grabbed him by the arm, separated him from his whisky, left the door standing open for Eve Trask, and yanked him out into the hall. He had his shoes in his hand. We didn't bother to wait for the elevator, and I pushed him from landing to landing down the stairs, hollering in his ear. He complained bitterly.

"Take it easy, Doc. I ain't too sober. How am I supposed to know you lose a cat? Wait a minute, can'tcha?"

"Nobody in his right mind would pass up a beautiful Siamese queen in the—"

"Queen? What's with this queen business?"

"Adult female—breeding stock." I shuddered at the thought. We pulled out of the lobby and into Forty-eighth.

"The cat she was with sure wasn't any king—common old alley cat. They were huntin' rats back of the restaurant." Elegant tried to sit on the curb. I didn't realize he wanted to shoe himself, and pulled him across the street. Rat hunting! They were probably hunting a quiet—

"Right here, Doc—by this cellar window." He didn't take a chance on sitting down again, but pulled his shoes on standing up. We skirted around each side of the building then plunged down into the cellar.

The best we could find was a pinch of her priceless fawn coat caught in the rough wood of a window frame. We crawled back into the apartment and I made myself a drink—haunted by visions of an enraged Katie that made Eve Trask look like Whistler's Mother.

17

I told Elegant Johnson what had happened to Trask and cautioned him to avoid contact with Marsh or any other cop, until I'd had a chance to square myself. He held his head under the kitchen sink faucet, cold, for several minutes while he thought it over.

"What sort of a joint is this Venturia, Doc?"

"Casual—pretty third-rate. Lot of young couples and what not. Why?"

"Old?"

"Yeah. Very." I couldn't figure his angle. "You thinking of going visiting?"

He shrugged into his coat; left the collar up. "You told me young Mallo was prowling around his brother's apartment the night before the Trask woman."

"That's right, and he got what he was looking for."

"But, next night, she *didn't* get what she was lookin' for. That correct? She was still askin' you questions after she'd searched the place?"

"Right again. Mickey's got that envelope."

"Maybe." He shoved his hat on his head. "Then, again, maybe he's up there trying to digest a couple of small-caliber slugs and has lost his envelope."

"He was at the track all morning—might still be there—but go ahead and nose around. Eve Trask is about due, and Marsh could turn up any time. You're just as well out of it. Call me before you come back."

"Right." He lanked off to the door, and the buzzer sounded, I told Elegant to take the stairway, and punched the latch. I stood in the hall while the elevator got started.

Eve came in looking pretty wild. "Where is he, Doc? Have you heard anything more?"

I hauled her into the apartment. "Hold everything a minute and listen to me, Eve. Will you listen?"

She stood hard fast, and her eyes didn't waver. "Is he dead, Doc?"

"Will you listen to me?" I steered her to a chair.

"Yes." Less bold now. "I'll do anything you say."

"All right. There's nothing in the world you can do for Huck right now. Sit down." She sat on the edge of the chair, stiffly erect. "I'm going to call the hospital, and I think we'll find he's alive. He'll probably be unconscious so he wouldn't know you, even if they'd let you see him. The only thing you can do is to let down a little and wait it out. Is that clear, Eve?"

She relaxed a little and said, "Yes." I felt sorry for her, but my pity didn't prevent me from remembering that she might have lost her tension when she learned that her husband probably wouldn't do any talking.

I dialed Huck's office number, gave my name, and asked who was speaking.

"Enders, Doc. The convention is still on. Want Lieutenant Marsh?"

"Yes, if you can get him away from the luminaries."

"Right. I'll flag him down."

Eddie came on after an interval of background sound effects. "Yeah, Doc. Make it fast."

"What about Trask?"

"Probable skull fracture. The wound shows no penetration on first examination. They say there's no reason why he shouldn't live—unless—you know—shock and stuff."

"Thanks. I'm in touch with Mrs. Trask. She'll be happy to hear it." I smiled over at Eve. She sat frozen with attention—or something else. I had a momentary flare of anger. "Anything new, Eddie?"

"A shell, for one thing. In a wastebasket, but apparently not thrown there because the other two must have been carried away. When we get the gun we'll know it."

"How about—auditory—indications?"

"The Trask woman there with you?"

"Yes—"

"She fit to talk?"

"Not too soon. See me first. You'll make more sense afterward."

"O.K., mastermind. About your auditory evidence, nobody seems to have heard the shots. It was a twenty-five automatic. The walls are thick and there's a punch press working in a loft next door. You can make as much noise as that gun with a ruler on a desk."

"No time, then?"

"The blood looked like a couple of hours or more old." He grumbled something that wasn't intended for me. Then he said, "Thank you, madam, I'll let you know as soon as I have word from the hospital." Hung up.

I turned to the woman. She was staring intently at me. "Huck will be all right, Eve. He was shot twice—in the shoulder and the head—"

"The head." It was neither a question nor an exclamation. It was a simple statement, as if in accompaniment to an unspoken thought. "That's why he's unconscious."

"That's right." I decided to give her further opportunity to declare herself. "There's the possibility of a skull fracture. They don't know yet. That might, of course, keep him unconscious for some time."

"How long?"

"It depends on a lot of things, Eve. He might not be—perfectly rational for a number of days."

"I see." She looked around her as though she had, just then, realized where she was. She stood up. "If you'll tell me where Huck is, I'd like to go now."

"Marsh hasn't told me yet. He's still pretty busy. I'll let you know at once." She moved thoughtfully, her tow-head down, hand on her chin. I followed her to the door. I said, "You'll be home?"

She looked up suddenly. "Of course."

"I'll call you there within the next half hour. Eddie Marsh will want to talk to you—as soon as you're up to it."

"I'm sure he will." The woman half smiled and went into the hall. "Thank you, Doc. I'm sorry you've been involved in this. You were very kind not to—misinterpret some of the things I've done to—avoid it." She spoke very quietly, and her gray-blue eyes were serious. "I think you'll have no further trouble."

The elevator came, and she offered her hand quite formally. I got the disturbing feeling I shouldn't let her get away.

"You're—going to be all right about this, Eve? I hate to have you go back to sweat it out alone."

This time she smiled, very nicely. "I'm greatly relieved."

She got into the elevator and was gone. I didn't know, as I stood there, whether I'd just heard a weary, hopeless confession of murder or the resignation of a woman who was giving up something she'd very much wanted to accomplish.

I went back into the apartment feeling very sorry for the woman who had conked me with a blunt object, stuck a nasty little gun in my belly, locked me in a closet, and probably had tried her best to kill her husband! I am not a very objective guy.

Johnny Mallo's murder seemed a long way off. Eddie Marsh had something, now, that he could get his teeth into. Even if it didn't turn out to be a homicide, it was a nice, routine piece of police business. They had all the good, substantial properties with which such dramas are garnished—bullets, bloodstains, a missing weapon, and a fine, politically nourishing backdrop of illegal gambling. Every change in the victim's faltering pulses caused an official hand to waver between two stacks of forms which would determine the charges and handling.

And Eve Trask had left without asking me if anybody knew who'd shot her husband! It might have been a difficult subject—for both of us.

I was pretty well upset over the prospect of my interview with Eddie, and three unproductive cat calls didn't help any.

Finally Elegant Johnson telephoned and said he'd got hold of Mickey Mallo. I told him to sneak into the office side and, in case the apartment was full of cops or something, to wait there.

Lorry called; asked if I'd heard anything new.

I said, "Have you?"

"I've been vegetating out here in the country. You never—"

"Were you vegetating out there this morning—say toward noon?"

"Why would you ask that? I did some shopping—"

"Where?"

"In Kew Gardens—I brought the Buick out with me. I like to drive around on the island. It's so beautiful."

"Were you driving around long?"

"Doc! What's *happened?* Why are you asking me all these questions?"

"Because somebody shot Huck Trask in his office a couple of hours ago."

"Somebody shot—" She was silent.

"Did you hear me, Lorry?"

"Oh—yes! It's shocking!" Her voice had a flat quality I couldn't interpret. It might have meant anything. *"Huck* Trask! Who killed him, Doc?"

Maybe that required some interpretation. "Nobody killed him, but somebody made a damned good try. He'll probably live."

It seemed to me she had some trouble getting out with, "Oh, I'm so glad!" Then, "But of course he can tell you who—hurt him, can't he?"

"Not yet, anyway. Listen, Lorry, I think you'd better come into town this afternoon."

"Why—" Panic? Fear of some sort of attack? How can you tell? "Yes, Doc. I'll come in right away. I could be there in an hour or so."

"Don't come here. Go home. I want to see you before the police start asking you questions."

"The police?" She almost whispered it.

"Naturally. It's bound to have something to do with Johnny's death. Everybody concerned will have to be questioned again." Probably not so politely, this time, it occurred to me. "Incidentally, I have some money that I think belongs to you."

"Money?" She laughed merrily. "This is a surprise! How much?"

"Quite a lot. I thought it might brighten your trip in if I told you."

"It does—definitely." It would, definitely. "Has the insurance company finally decided—"

"No. It's five thousand dollars"—I heard her gasp—"and I think it's the reason Huck Trask was shot. That's why you'll have to answer a lot of questions." The other gasp was just a warm-up. Lorry was a very unhappy young woman. I had no doubt, however, that she'd be in to claim the dough. She'd have gone into a cage of lions for it.

I heard the elevator door, then steps down the hall to the office door. When I went through I found Elegant and Mickey Mallo. The boy looked scared as hell. He said, "'What's this for?"

"Sit down." They found chairs, and I sat on the desk. "It's a mean spot, Mick." I glanced at Elegant, and he shook his head. "Detective Johnson hasn't told you, but Huck Trask has been shot."

Mallo said something under his breath; began reaching for cigarettes, staring at the floor as he groped. Finally he said, "What's that got to do with me?"

"I don't know—exactly." I put on the beard. "Of course the Nautilus fix will probably have to be brought out—"

That woke him up. "Why? Huck didn't have anything to do with it."

"He didn't?"

"No."

"All right, Mick. So he didn't. Alan Copey doesn't know that."

The boy lifted his head; looked like somebody'd hit him. "Where did you get that?"

"He squawked."

"To the cops?"

"Not yet. He will when he hears about this. How many other marks did you take, Mallo?"

He went sullen. "Nobody."

"You sent out only one note with Trask's cards?"

"Two. I sent two. The other guy didn't go along."

"Ralph Pack?"

Mickey stood up suddenly. Elegant leaned over and took hold of him. "Let go of me, goddammit! You can't keep me here. I'm leaving!"

"Sure. You can go. Whenever you want." Elegant let him loose. "I thought I might be able to keep you out of jail."

He glared at me; went suspicious. "How?"

"You told me you'd talk about Johnny's deal with Trask as soon as you were sure you wouldn't hurt anybody. Remember? *Hurt* anybody!" I hammed over to the door. "Come on, Elegant. This punk can rot in jail as far as I'm concerned."

"It wasn't Huck I was afraid of hurting, Doc—honest. I didn't know anything would happen to him. I only—"

"Who did you think something was going to happen to then?"

He squirmed. "Look, Doc. I was going to tell you. Who's this detective? A racing cop?"

"Mr. Johnson is a private detective—in my employ."

The long man got up. "You don't need me for this." He sauntered into the apartment. I thought of my Forester too late. I closed the door and faced the kid.

"What time did you leave the track, Mick?"

"About ten. What's this about Huck?"

I roughed it out for him. "Can you account for yourself through that period? Don't tell me you were home. You weren't."

"I was around town."

"Better make it good when Eddie Marsh starts working on you. He'll want to know where you were and who saw you there." He gulped a couple of times and didn't say anything. "Where's Trask's envelope?"

He reached into his pocket and handed me a brown manila packet with a rubber band around it. It contained a letter of agreement—a well-drawn partnership between Mallo and Trask in an enterprise to be known as *Trask Publications*. It involved a matter of seventy-five hundred dollars and 25 per cent of the weekly gross. Johnny had a nice investment if he could face himself mornings. There was a record of twenty-five hundred dollars which had been paid by Trask. The balance was represented by a demand note for five thousand. This Johnny had neatly canceled and added "Paid in Full."

"Apparently Johnny had intended to deliver this to Trask, Mickey."

"He promised to—the morning after he died."

"How do you know?"

"I heard him. Huck gave him the money that night at the office and called me in to witness some kind of a receipt. Johnny claimed he had the papers locked up and would get them in the morning."

"Was it a friendly meeting?"

"They didn't like each other."

"What time was this on Friday night?"

"About ten o'clock or so."

"Did you leave with Johnny?"

"No. He said he had to go home and make weight. I left at the same time, but not with Johnny."

"Did you see your brother again that night?"

"Not—to talk to."

"What do you mean by that? You saw him again?"

"Yes."

"Where? When?"

"In front of his apartment building. I got to thinking after he left Huck's office and wanted to get my—betting slip back. I was going to square up with him. He didn't have any right to tell *me* what to do when, all the time, he was—"

"Why didn't you talk to him that night?"

"He was with somebody. They went on in—"

"Who was he with, Mick?"

"Eve Trask."

18

Mickey Mallo had been gone an hour, and I'd sent Elegant John-son off to stake out at the Johnny Mallo apartment, when Eddie got here. The big guy seemed tired.

"How about a drink, Commissioner?"

He collapsed into a chair and threw his hat on the couch. "No drink, thanks. I've got hours more to go. The brains and talent are really knocking on me."

"How's Trask?"

"He's—rallied. I think that's the word they used. No frac-ture, apparently. They tell me, unofficially, that he'll probably live."

"Unconscious; of course—"

"Quite. I've got a team of harpies worrying about that, you know—the first time, the poor gent opens his eyes I'm to holler 'who killed you, pal?' at him. Then the case is closed."

"I've got a couple of ladies worrying about it too."

"Yeah?"

"Yeah. Both Mrs. Trask and Mrs. Mallo are displaying more than casual interest in Trask's ability to talk."

"Each waiting for him to tell us the other one did it?"

"It could be that way. It could be a lot of other ways too. Lorry could be worrying because she thinks Ralph Pack did it. Eve Trask could be worrying—"

"What about Pack?"

I told Eddie, in detail, about the Nautilus affair; about the physician's receiving Mickey's note with his Wednesday copy of *Huck's Hot Horses,* and his apparent relationship with Sam Fenner.

Eddie peered at me suspiciously, but, so far, pleasantly. "That's helpful, if not very important. You say Pack was a subscriber to Trask's service?"

"He was."

"Trask must have covered him up. He wasn't on the list."

I did an internal broad jump. "The hell he wasn't!"

"No. We went over it carefully. It's a typical sucker list." Eddie dropped the subject casually, and I decided I'd better do some investigating before I said anything more.

"What else have you learned, Doc? As you know, I take a pretty dim view of your one-man crime crusades. Now that this thing has become a definite police matter I'm going to damned well see that you don't foul me up."

"You told me to go get a couple of facts. I got them. It doesn't do any good for you to go cop on me."

He laughed—the last time I saw him laugh that day. "All right, all right. I won't go official if you don't go prima donna. Let's go back where you left off. Why would Eve Trask be worrying about her husband's recovering consciousness?"

"Because there's a pretty good chance she shot him herself."

Marsh was straight up in his chair at once. "What've you got?"

Here would be the pay-off. The water looked cold as hell, and I hated to take the plunge. "I've got a couple of facts, dammit—and you're going to be sore as a goat. I was sorry for the woman and held off—"

Eddie got up and paced across the room. "Doc! Don't stall! Let's have it. This has got to be tied up with the Mallo-Nembutal thing and I'll look terrible downtown anyway."

I told him what I knew—about Mickey's search on Monday night, Eve's on Tuesday; about the gun, the letter, and the five thousand dollars. He listened without interruption, getting angrier as I went along. When I got to Mick Mallo's story about Eve and Johnny, he went out into the kitchen and brought back my Forester bottle and ice. I didn't say anything until he'd set the stuff up on the table.

"Is that a gesture of friendship? Or are you going to drink my liquor and then beat me about the head and neck?"

Marsh poured a couple of drinks and glowered. "It's both. The kindest gesture I could make, right now, would be to get drunk and beat you privately." He handed me my glass and sat down. "I thought I had work to do elsewhere. It seems that most of it is right here. Now; what have you made of all this?"

"Absolutely nothing, so far. Eve Trask is certainly guilty of armed entry or something. Mickey could be prosecuted for attempted fraud." I was glad I hadn't mentioned Lorry's switch episode—another attempted fraud. "You could damned near ruin Pack with ridicule too. But as far as the Johnny Mallo murder—and it was a murder—as far as that's concerned, you're still a long way off."

"You're certain it was a small-caliber automatic the Trask woman had on you?"

"Absolutely. I saw it full in the flashlight beam."

"Trask was shot with a twenty-five Colt—at least from the center-fire and the action marks on the shell, Enders figured it for a Colt—"

"It had the characteristic barrel shape."

Eddie shoved his feet out in front of him, lay back in the chair. "Doc, I suppose there's no question about Mallo's having been killed with the drug—by means of it?"

"None whatever, in my opinion."

"It couldn't have been taken in ignorance and be balling up all our thinking?"

"It *could* have, of course, but that would make an unbelievable coincidence out of the whole thing. You can't say that Johnny's accidental death started all this either. It had started before he died."

"But why would Eve Trask enter into a conspiracy with her old flame, Johnny, meet him after Trask had settled his debt, kill him, and then, a few days later, shoot Trask?"

"I haven't the foggiest idea. I didn't learn of her visit to Mallo until an hour ago. There's one thing sure. If her errand to Johnny's place that night was friendly, she wouldn't have killed him. If it was unfriendly, she wouldn't have killed her husband."

Eddie clinked the ice in his glass. "The Nembutal business was too sly, knowing, smart, Doc; and the Trask shooting too sloppy. I'm sticking to physical evidence. We got a lot of it, and your—confessions make it look good. I'll pick up the Trask woman for questioning."

"Of course. Lorry Mallo is coming to town today—for her dough—and I've got a hunch she can give you something. The Trask shooting may have taken some sort of pressure off her."

"Like what?"

"I don't know. Maybe something to do with Ralph Pack. She's been scared as hell about something. She ran off the night Mallo was killed—possibly knowing about the meeting he would have that evening with Trask—and she got out of town the minute she could after the funeral."

"I want to know where she was this morning. Let the Mallo thing take care of itself."

"She was shopping on Long Island—so she says. She'll be at her apartment this evening. I dangled the five thousand, and she came running. There's a little lady as loves a buck."

"How about her for the Mallo business—insurance motive?"

"Perfect. What did you call the Nembutal idea—knowing, smart? If Lorry Mallo is smart, I'm Socrates."

"She could have been coached—"

"Pack? Maybe, but he'd be too smart himself to deal her in. He'd know the law, and, what's more, he'd know something about insurance. Hell, Eddie! the Mallo girl was on the run *before* her husband was killed."

"We'll worry about her later. The Trask woman looks like a sitting duck, although I can't figure why. I want that gun, and I'm going after it. I should have all the laboratory stuff shortly." Eddie drained his glass and got up. "Thanks for the drink. I'm officially off duty until tomorrow now."

"Don't apologize. Just remember that your judgment isn't to be trusted for twelve hours."

Marsh frowned. "I wish to heaven yours was a little sounder. If you do any more prowling around on this will you, for the love of mike, keep me informed?"

"Yes, sir. Thanks for being so tolerant."

"Don't ask me why. I'll call you."

"Where's Trask?"

"Bellevue."

"You got somebody staked out on his door?"

"Night and day. We don't like people knocked off while they're guests of the city."

"Very sensible." Marsh started for the entry. "You're sure Pack's name wasn't on Trask's list—wasn't in his file?"

"Sure. I went over the files myself. It wasn't there. Why?"

"It was there yesterday. I was wondering why Trask—"

"How do you know it was there yesterday?" All cop.

"I peeked."

I thought, for a moment, I was in for it, but Marsh gave me a hard look and went out to the elevator. "Go and peek at Lorry Mallo. It's more interesting and might just keep you out of circulation for a while."

I went back and finished my highball. Eve Trask called and I told her where Huck was. I wanted to tell her that I'd had to report our clash, but made excuses to myself and didn't do it.

I got out the Mallo-Trask letter of agreement again and studied it. Johnny had made a tough deal—one which would have kept Huck in virtual slavery. Twenty-five per cent of the gross would probably be equal to half, at least, of the net profit even in that business. To make a fair living and retire seventy-five hundred dollars from a standing start could have been quite a struggle under conditions like that.

Eddie had studied the document and made no comment beyond suggesting that I should not let it out of my possession until Trask recovered.

It was some time before Lorry called and announced she was at home. I got the money out of the file and went over. She met

me at the door with proper concern for the guy her husband
had hated.

"How is Huck Trask, Doc—have you heard?"

"He was badly hurt, Lorry. He'll probably live." I followed
her into the living room. We sat down. The redhead managed
an almost sympathetic look.

"And you say it was about some *money* or something?"

Of course I screamed. It wasn't nice of me to laugh, but the
way she read the line killed me.

"What's so funny?"

"I'm sorry. You never know what's funny until it happens to
you."

She drew herself up and gave me the duchess. "I fail to
see—"

"Look, Lorry, you're wonderful! You're beautiful! I practically love you, youngster, but you sure do have a lot of respect
for a buck. You made those big, sorrowful eyes over a guy you
probably disliked intensely and practically searched my pockets
with them at the same time. Here." I dug into my coat and came
up with the envelope of bills.

She thumbed them over; smiled. "I think I can forgive you,
Doc. Aren't they *beautiful?* Where did they come from?"

"From Huck Trask. He owed the money to Johnny."

"Johnny had this money with him—that night?"

"That's right. He taped it to the bottom of the rubbing-
table drawer. I suppose it was he. You didn't, did you?"

"No." She stared across the room. "No, Doc, I didn't. Johnny did. He wasn't going to let me know about it. That's the
most money I've ever seen—any time—except maybe in a bank.
You don't think how much it is then, like in a bank. But I think
how much it is *now*—now that I know Johnny hid it from me—"

"He was probably just putting it away for safekeeping. Don't
try to make something of it." She didn't look up; shook her
head slowly.

"No, Doc. That money was for a very special purpose. You
should have some idea, by this time."

"Something to do with gambling?"

"You mean on horses? Johnny Mallo? Never!" She looked straight at me with those blue eyes hard as sapphire. "No. That money was for the one kind of play my husband was a sucker for. A woman."

"Eve?"

"You saw the wire, didn't you?"

"Is that all you base it on?"

"Doc, listen. Johnny Mallo knew that if I ever got my hands on this much money I'd leave him. You think I'm money hungry? I am. I have been for more than three years. I never realized how much nasty, brutal difference money could mean between two supposedly normal people."

"If it was as bad as that, why didn't you get a job? You earned your living long enough to—"

"Sure! Sure I could have gotten a job—any time. I could have run off with another man, too, if I'd wanted. I helped earn every dime of that money—of all the money Johnny made. I took it for granted we were partners in some sort of a life effort. I—" She put her flaming head against the back of the chair, her arm over her eyes. "I don't know why I'm saying these things."

"There isn't much else to do, kid. You can't save anybody's feelings now."

"Feelings?" She sat up straight again. "I'm not trying to save anybody's feelings! For three years my husband made excuses to see that woman. Almost every week he'd meet her—always at night, Doc. Mickey told me about it first, then one night I followed him. It was like Mickey said—they met at the office. Huck Trask was never there." Her red mouth made a hard rectangle. "And I should spare somebody's feelings?"

"Did you know that Johnny and Trask were in partnership in *Huck's Hot Horses?*"

Her eyes widened. "No." Narrowed. "They hated each other. It was an excuse to see Eve."

"They didn't hate each other in Florida. It started there."

"Everything started there. It's never stopped." Lorry stared vacantly out the window. "Was the five thousand dollars because of the partnership?"

"Yes. The final payment."

"Oh no!" She didn't raise her voice or stop looking out the window. "Not the *final* payment, Doc."

I let it go at that. If this kid ever tangled with Eve Trask they should put it on in the Garden. We sat awhile without saying anything. My few facts began to piece themselves together— Johnny sees Eve at eight o'clock, Pack about nine, and Trask a little before ten. He gets the cash from Trask, meets Eve, goes to the apartment. Did Trask turn up there later?

It could have been that way. Huck had heard Johnny say he was going home to make weight and probably was long familiar with his routine. The Nembutal idea wasn't a spur-of-the-moment method, and the killer was prepared to execute his plan long ahead. Certainly husband-killing-wife's-lover is nothing new in motivation, and that would let Eve shoot Trask with considerable motivation of her own. That, also, would leave the tidy crime of calculated revenge in the hands of a guy who made his living calculating, and the sloppy, infuriated shooting in the hands of a woman whose fury I'd sampled.

At any rate, it was the first theory that seemed to fit all the facts.

Lorry stirred in her chair with a small moan. She'd been crying and had mascara on her cheeks. I said, "I'm sorry, kid. It isn't a very pretty story any way you look at it. Don't get yourself into any more trouble. I think Eve Trask will be quite busy with the police for some time. They seem to think she shot her husband."

"They've found that out?"

"Not exactly yet, but it looks like they might. By the way. Do you happen to know if any of the bunch owned a little Colt automatic—a twenty-five?"

"Why, yes. Johnny's had one for years. I'd almost forgotten. I haven't seen it around for a long time. We used it—all of us used it for target practice in Florida."

19

As I turned the corner away from the building, Elegant Johnson stepped out of the alley. I'd forgotten, for the moment, that I'd staked him out there.

"She had a caller ahead of you, Doc."

"Yeah? Who?"

"The kid—Mickey—twenty minutes before you turned up. He came out after nine minutes, in a hell of a hurry. Flagged a cab and beat it."

"He's in and out of there all the time. It needn't mean anything. How long after she got home did he get here?"

"She hadn't been in the place ten minutes."

"Maybe she called him from the outside." If he'd been at the Venturia, it would have taken him longer than ten minutes. "Incidentally, did you notice if he had a key? Or did he ring the bell?"

"He rang her apartment."

Elegant's long face creased up like a weather map. He was obviously waiting for professional approval. "Were you looking over his shoulder? He knows you by sight."

"Well, you see, it was this way. I figured you'd want to know which place people were ringing, so I found me a little car grease in the street and smeared some on the button. The little man come in neat as pie, then rubbed off his thumb on his handkerchief while he was waiting for the latch."

"Cute. Have you had anything to eat?"

"Yeah. I'm good for several hours if you want me to stick."

"I do. If Mrs. Mallo goes out, don't lose her. I want to know where she goes."

"I've got my car up the block."

"Good. Now there's another thing. It could be pretty important. If Mrs. Trask— You know her by sight, don't you?"

"I made it a point to. I know 'em all."

"If Mrs. Trask comes here, don't let *her* out of your sight. Follow her upstairs into the apartment. Tell them anything you can think of that will keep you with them. Then get hold of me."

"You think the Trask woman might start something?"

"I think she's already started something she may not be able to finish. Keep your eye peeled for a dirty little twenty-five automatic—"

"It's that bad?"

"I don't know. Maybe. But I do know if those two women ever get into that apartment alone, the roof'll blow off."

"O.K., Doc. I might have to raise a lot of hell. It won't look too good downtown—"

"Stick around, Elegant. You'll look wonderful downtown before this is over."

He gave me a skeptical leer and went back to his post. I walked over to my place and found a city car parked in front. There were a couple of cops in it. As I approached the entry one of them got out.

"Dr. Connor?"

"Yes."

"We're supposed to take you to Bellevue—Lieutenant Marsh's orders."

He opened the rear door and I got in. "You know anything about it?"

"No." He slammed the door and got back under the wheel. "He only said get you."

He growled the siren and whooped out into Forty-eighth. Trask would be conscious—or dying. I poked the second man on the shoulder. "How long you fellows been waiting?"

"Ten, fifteen minutes—maybe fifteen minutes since we got the call." He looked at his book and his watch. "Sixteen." He put his reference materials back with something of a gesture. "I got a good sense of time."

The driver used his brakes for the first time on the run. "Here you are, sir."

"And a very good thing, too, officer. Thanks for missing everything." I piled out and scrambled into the office and got a room number. Eddie was waiting at the floor desk. He looked harassed.

"Trask is conscious, Doc, but he's not doing any talking. He wants to see you."

"Did he say why?"

"No. He says nothing that makes any sense. He's using his condition to stall—" Eddie led off down the corridor. "Come on."

The door carried the "No Visitors" card, and there was a uniformed cop sitting in a chair by it, reading a book. He stood up as Marsh came along.

"You can go for a smoke if you want, Flynn. We'll be here ten minutes or so." The man thanked him and left. "Maybe you'd better go in alone, Doc; the guy's afraid of me."

I went in. Trask was lying on his left side, his head pretty well covered with bandages. He opened his eyes.

"Hello, Doc."

"Hello, Huck. They tell me you're feeling better."

"Yeah. That's what they tell me too. Sit down, will you?"

I pulled up a chair. "What can I do to help, Huck. Marsh said you wanted to see me."

The man closed his eyes again, stirred stiffly in the bed. "I don't know what you can do, Doc. But I did want to see you. Marsh can only make trouble. That's his job—"

He struggled his left arm from under him and put his hand on my knee. "Have you seen Eve?"

"Yes. I've seen her; talked with her."

"What—where was she when this happened to me?"

I said very gently, "Don't you think you'd better tell me why that's important, Huck?"

"Doc, if you're willing to help me, you'll have to do it my way. Otherwise— *Please* do it my way, fella." He took his hand off my knee and covered his eyes.

"All right. I'll go as far as I can. You talk as though you didn't know who shot you—or that you didn't *want* to—"

Trask lay silent for some time, his face averted, strained; sweat on his neck. "I don't know, Doc. I heard the outer door open—the one to the hall. I thought it was Eve and didn't look up. That's all."

"Someone fired from the anteroom, then?"

"I suppose so. I don't know."

It could have been the truth. Only one of the shells had been found in the office. The first two could have been fired from the outer room. The man on the bed eased himself over on his back. I crossed his pillows and settled him down. He wasn't in shape to do much more talking.

I said, "Eve was at the track distributing the card when I heard from her, Huck. The crew boss had called her. She tried to reach you at the office. You were probably unconscious."

"She put out the card, eh?" He smiled a little.

"Yes."

"Good kid—know it, Doc?"

"The best. Why do you suspect her of shooting you?"

He continued to smile. "I don't. She'd have shot me years ago—"

"Marsh thinks she did it, Huck."

"I thought as much. He talked that way." Trask moved his head with some effort. "Why does he think so?"

"The gun—a twenty-five Colt automatic. I know that Eve was—familiar with it."

Trask reached for the corner of a sheet and mopped his neck with it, "A twenty-five Colt—Johnny Mallo's little gun?"

"They think so."

The man was very pale. "We all were familiar with it. Mickey used to borrow it once in a while to take out in the woods."

"I'm afraid he didn't borrow it this time." A nurse poked her head in the door and went away. "Huck, listen. You shouldn't talk much longer. Do you know any possible reason why Eve should try to kill you?"

He smiled, a tight, hard movement of his mouth as though his pain had suddenly become worse. "No." He twisted his head away from me. "Will you go now, Doc? There isn't anything you can do, I'm afraid—thinking the way you are—"

"All right, Huck." I got up, leaned over, and put my hand over his. "I want you to know one thing though. Johnny had canceled your note and the letter of agreement. I have them."

"You knew about that?" He faced me again.

"I do now. I know how hard Mallo pressed you these last few years—what a rough deal he made."

"That's over now, Doc." Trask pulled his hand away and put it over his eyes. "Thanks for your help."

"There's something else, isn't there? You wanted me for something else—maybe thought you couldn't trust me with it?"

He put his hand down and stared at the ceiling. "Yes. There's something else. I didn't want to discuss it with Marsh—I'm not sure enough about it. Have you changed your mind about Johnny's death—as to how he died?"

"No. He was murdered."

The man on the bed was quiet for what seemed a long time. "I won't ask you how, Doc—I'm quite sure I know—"

I grabbed my excitement and throttled it. "And somebody shot you for it?"

"I—don't know. I can't believe it."

"Tell me about it."

The guy looked pretty green; the sweat stood on his neck again. His words pulled themselves loose one at a time. I knew I should go.

"A prescription, Doc—a prescription for weight reducing. Benzedrine to curb appetite. Nembutal to overcome the sleeplessness caused by the Benzedrine, sweat baths, too, Doc—sweat baths and a warning—"

"When was this?"

Trask seemed to be struggling to stay conscious. "Some years ago."

"Did Pack give the prescriptions?"

"No—I can't remember the doctor's name. In Florida—"

"Who were they for, Huck?"

His hand moved toward his face; fell back. "Oh, God! Doc! Doc, you've got to help us. It couldn't have been Eve. She couldn't have done this to me!"

Then he fainted. I hurried out to the desk and suggested that somebody see him at once. A long-legged young resident who'd been looking at some charts took off for the room. Eddie Marsh came over to me.

"Get anything?"

"Yes. I pushed him too far getting it, though. You'll have to let him alone for a day or two."

"All right. What'd he tell you?"

"He's afraid Eve shot him. It seems that she knew something about the danger of sweat baths and sleeping drugs—apparently the lady has always had to watch her figure."

"So Trask makes a guess when Mallo dies in the bath, and she has to stop him. Wasn't she supposed to be in love with Mallo?"

"Mrs. Mallo thinks so, but Eve's attitude in talking to me was that she hated his guts." I went back to her statement that Johnny's character was a matter of opinion. "It could be both ways, of course."

"Sure. Get complicated. It's more fun that way." Marsh grunted it out and walked off to give Flynn some instructions. When he came back he said, "I'll have the Trask woman picked up. You going home?"

"No. Will you drop me off at the Venturia? I want to talk to young Mallo."

The idea pulled him away from the casual business of getting his hat. "What about?"

"About his professional future."

"Has he got a professional future?"

"He could have. I've got a hunch he won't ask for any more trouble. The boy took an awful pushing around, apparently, and got sick of it." He and his redheaded sister-in-law! "I've also got a hunch there was another bet going on Nautilus last Friday—maybe a big one."

"Who would have made it, Doc?"

"The person who probably put Mickey up to killing off the favorite—the beautiful, stupid, money-hungry widow."

"She could have killed her husband too." Marsh shoved his hat on his head and started down the hall. "She and young Mallo make as good a triangle as any of 'em."

"Sure she could have killed her husband." I remembered the dull business about the switch again. Only a complete moron could have engineered it. "But not if she could have wheedled somebody else into doing it for her."

On the way across town Eddie was quiet. Finally he said, "Lorry Mallo's story checks completely, Doc. Her husband told her he was going out so she made plans to visit her friend and left. Mallo was still in the apartment. She claims she didn't have any idea where he was going—that she didn't know about the telegram until after Mallo was dead."

"I'm quite sure she didn't."

"Why?"

"I think she would have followed him—maybe made a scene. She was pretty well fed up with Eve Trask." At the same time, I was thinking that Lorry undoubtedly suspected where Johnny was going that night. Her state of mind would hardly let her think anything else. "But maybe you're right, Eddie. I could be making it too complicated."

Marsh laughed. "Wishful thinking, Doc. You like 'em complicated." We pulled up in front of the Venturia. "They're all simple enough—when you get the deadwood out of the way. When'll I see you?"

"Give me a call when you've picked up Eve Trask. I'm very anxious to know what she has to say."

"I'll do that. You might work your young jockey friend for a hot tip."

As the police car drove down the street I decided that I might, at that.

20

I got Mickey's number off the mailbox and took a look at the electric latch. It was worn and loose. There was a gap between the door and the frame. My thin safe-deposit-box key slipped easily through to the latch and pried it back. I went in, walked up the stairway to the third floor, and found 3-D.

There were men's voices in the apartment. I stood and listened. Mallo was speaking angrily, his speech tense, hoarse.

"And there's another thing you'd better not forget. If any of it comes out, all of it does. I'll see to that—I'll lay it right on the line for anybody that asks me." There was a short silence. Somebody walked stiffly across the room. "Then you're cooked—but good."

The other man spoke quietly. He was near the door. "There's little likelihood of any of it coming out, if you use your head, Mickey. Nobody but Connor thinks your brother was murdered. The police have no grounds whatever to continue their investigation—"

"Johnny died from an accident. There was something the matter with the electric switch in the sweatbox. Lorry told me Connor looked at it." Mickey's voice came closer to the door. "But the cops are going to get plenty curious to know who shot Huck Trask."

"Trask? Shot?"

"That's right, smart guy. He's dying in the hospital right now—shot in the head." Mallo's tone got very unpleasant;

threatening. "Right now the cops are digging into those files, and guess whose name they'll dig up?"

"Damn you, you told me you'd get my name out of there!" It was Ralph Pack, of course. "Why didn't you do it?"

"I did."

"And destroyed it?"

"You think I'm nuts, Pack?"

"Where is it? I want it—right now." A quick, heavy step; a couple of scrambling noises. I expected a brawl—then Mickey's voice froze the sounds inside.

"Get out. Fast."

"You can't force me into such a—"

"Shut up and get out."

A hand moved the doorknob, and I retreated around a corner and waited. I watched Pack go the other way to the elevator and heard Mallo's door close again. I went back and knocked. After some delay the boy opened up and faced me across the threshold.

"Oh." He straightened out his angry face. "Hello, Doc."

He blocked the door, but I shoved in. "Did you have a gun on Pack just now?"

He backed off; said nothing. I bellied close to him. "Let's see that gun, Mallo."

"I've got no gun, Doc." His eyes were frightened. They flicked from side to side, looking for a hole. I grabbed a handful of shirt and yanked him to me. His right hand went to a pocket and started up with the gun. I took it away from him, put my hand on his chest, and shoved.

There it was in my hand—the little twenty-five automatic. I didn't have time to ask myself questions. Mallo came charging back across the room, gun or no gun. He stopped just out of reach.

"Hold it, Mick!"

"What are you going to do with that?"

"I'm going to turn it over to the police. They've been looking for it."

"It—was Johnny's."

"I know. Where did you get it—and when?" When he just stood there I said, "Did you get it at Lorry's apartment when you were there today?"

"No."

"Are you sure Lorry didn't give it to you?"

"Lorry didn't know it was still around. Johnny kept it hidden."

"Then where did you get the gun?"

"I had it all the time. I borrowed it from Johnny."

"If that's so, you shot Trask with it."

He was badly scared. "What do you mean?"

"This is the automatic that was used on Trask. There isn't a chance in a hundred for it not to be. Want to talk that over with the cops?"

The boy walked slowly and thoughtfully across the room and got a cigarette from a sideboard near what I took to be a bedroom door. He put the cigarette into his mouth and patted his pockets looking for a match. Then he took a step toward the door. As I said, "Wait a minute—here's a match," he blew. I raced after him, like a chump, and had a door slammed in my face. After I'd fallen over a chair and heard Mallo's feet pounding far down the hall, I gave it up.

The gun wasn't big enough to carry all the prints that would be on it by that time, but I dutifully carried it by the trigger guard to the kitchen and looked around for a small box and some string. A cigarette carton and the cord from the window shade made a neat, practically regulation package. Then I called Eddie Marsh. He wasn't at the office, so I rang Eve Trask's apartment. She answered.

"Oh, Doc. I have company."

"Marsh?"

"Yes. The lieutenant tells me Huck will be all right—that I can see him."

"I had a talk with Huck, Eve. I also had a talk with Lorry Mallo. Mickey saw you go into Johnny's apartment Friday night. Something that just happened makes me think you may not be as badly involved as I'd believed. I want to talk to Marsh. When

I get through, tell him where you found the gun you used to stick me up. It's the gun your husband was shot with and it looks like you did it."

"It was Johnny Mallo's gun. I found it that night—in a bureau drawer under some— Wait a minute—"

Marsh came on. "Maybe you don't think I'm competent to do my own work, Doc. What do you want of Mrs. Trask?"

"I just wanted to tell her that she could stop worrying about the twenty-five automatic. I've got it."

"*What?*" Not loud, but one of those nice, satisfactory long ones. "Where'd you find it?"

"I just took it away from a very mean little person named Mickey Mallo."

"What the hell was he doing with it? That doesn't make sense."

"He was threatening a physician named Pack with it. Not brandishing or anything; just for emphasis. I think you'd better pick the kid up."

"I think I'd better pick 'em all up. Where's that gun? Where are you now?"

"The gun's neatly packed on the table beside me. I'm at young Mallo's apartment."

"And where's he?"

"He is, as you would have it, at large."

"Get it down to the precinct. I'll meet you in ten minutes."

"Are you bringing Mrs. Trask in with you?"

"After what you've just told me? Are you kidding?"

"She knows—or could know—how Johnny Mallo was killed."

"That's not what interests me—at the moment. Get over to the precinct, will you?"

I said I would, and hung up. Johnny's murder was what interested me at the moment—whether Eddie Marsh liked it or not. Almost since the first, the group had divided itself sharply into two classes—the shrewd and the stupid. Pack, Eve, and maybe Huck Trask on one side—Lorry and Mickey Mallo on the other.

The Nembutal-sweatbath idea was anything but stupid, even if it had originated with the warning of some physician other than Pack. The man would have had no reason to suggest—or even to remember—that the evidence of such a death might never be discovered.

Yet, of all people, young Mickey had turned up with the little gun that seemed to be the key to the whole affair. Trask appeared to be out of it. Lorry Mallo might have turned the automatic over to her brother-in-law—but why? Unless they were associated in Johnny's murder, or something, it would have been unthinkably dull. Or would it have been characteristically dull? The possibility that the two crimes were not associated refused to stay seriously in my mind.

I took a quick look around the apartment—medicine cabinet, kitchen shelves, and what not—without finding anything helpful. Then I cabbed down and turned the gun in at the precinct. Marsh wasn't there yet and I didn't wait for him; left word to call me at home.

It was close to midnight—less than twelve hours since Trask had been shot. It could have been several days. Less than a week since Johnny Mallo had slept his life away in a sweatbath. It could have been a month.

I got ready for bed with the disturbing thought that maybe I couldn't see the trees for the forest. Equally disturbing, the idea that Katie might call. It was the first time I'd ever found myself hoping she wouldn't.

With my tired contact with cool, fresh sheets, the telephone rang. Elegant Johnson's habitual drawl was speeded up with whatever the guy uses for excitement.

"There's stuff going on over here, Doc. About ten minutes ago the Trask woman pulled up with a car and parked down the street from the entrance. She turned off her lights and just sat there—"

"Is she there now?"

"No. Wait a minute. The babe is gone—skipped."

"Lorry Mallo?"

"That's right. The minute I seen the woman settle down to wait, I carded the latch and went up to the Mallo apartment, trying to head off a brawl like you said. Mrs. Mallo had cleared out. She must've gone the back way."

"Or the fire escape."

"I could see the fire escape from where I was standing. Besides that, she went out in such a hurry she left the door standing open. I looked around to see if she'd packed or anything. I don't think she had."

"She probably saw Eve Trask drive up, Elegant. That would do it. You say Mrs. Trask is gone?"

"Yes. I think maybe she followed Mrs. Mallo on foot." He sounded like a kid who'd broken a window. "Her car's still here, but I can't find her prowling around any place. I'm sorry as hell, Doc."

I told him to forget it and go home.

There was enough light in the street for Lorry to have recognized Eve Trask or her car, and the Mallo apartment was not too high up in the building. More complexities kept crowding me. Mickey could have telephoned Lorry that I had the gun. Pack could have told her that Mickey was getting tough and might blow the works. Or she could have been just plain threatened by any of them. On the basis of my new forest-for-the-trees approach, I decided to think, simply, that she was scared of Eve Trask. Just as I was starting to swirl around in a lot of ill-assorted reasons why she should be afraid of Eve, Eddie Marsh called.

"Thanks for the gun, Doc. You needn't have bothered to pack it so carefully, there are no latent prints on it that are worth anything. Young Mallo will have a lot of explaining to do on possession alone. I've got a call out for him. This thing is beginning to wrap up. The gun'll do it."

"I hope so, Eddie. In the meantime, Eve Trask has been stalking Mrs. Mallo. I don't know what it means."

"Hell! They're all stalking each other. Let 'em alone. They all suspect each other—even the husband-and-wife team." The big lug made it seem very simple and practically smacked his lips over it. "Incidentally, have you still got that Boy Scout pistol the department let you have for being—helpful?"

"It's around some place. Why?"

"It mightn't be a bad idea to put it under your pillow. These people think you know more than you do."

"I've got a hunch I do."

"Do *what?* Are you nuts?"

"Yes. I am nuts. Strictly. And I've got a hunch I know more than I think I do."

Marsh growled. "Go to bed and get some rest. I wish to hell I could."

I told him that such was my pious intention, and wished him well with his little gun. Before he hung up he added, "Speaking of the little gun, Doc, the Trask woman claims she found it in Johnny Mallo's drawer—that she had every right to be there because she was protecting her friend Mrs. Mallo's interests; that she thought you were a burglar or she never would have *thought* of the gun. And guess what: that she left the gun in the apartment, and that you'll be happy to support all these statements! I just thought you'd be amused, or do you want to make an official complaint that she manhandled you?"

"I wouldn't think of it. But I am not amused. She's an unmitigated, if very good-natured, liar. If I make a complaint about her, it'll be murder."

"That'll be nice. Good night."

I felt silly getting my gun out of the desk drawer, but I did, and put the thing on the mantel. During a lull in the traffic I heard a cat yowl outside. I pulled on some clothes and rushed down to explore the alleys. My gray tom friend was sitting alone back of the restaurant kitchen looking pretty forlorn. A lot of groping and stumbling over trash cans produced nothing for either of us.

I emerged from the alley just in time to see a familiar figure—a woman—slip out of the darkness into the entrance of my apartment. It was Lorry Mallo. She glanced at the row of mailboxes and reached for the button. I looked around for Eve Trask, failed to see her any place, and crossed the street. Lorry looked up as I approached her and let out a small scream.

"Doc! Let me in—*please—quick!*"

I opened the door and pushed her ahead of me into the elevator, which somebody, for once, had left on the ground floor. "What's the trouble?"

"I've been followed. I'm terribly afraid—"

"Eve Trask?" I pushed the button, and we clanked upward.

"Yes—oh, *yes!* She wants to kill me!" Lorry watched the lobby disappear below and sank down on the little stool. "You didn't see her outside anywhere, did you?"

"No. I looked around for her as soon as I saw you in the entrance."

The blue eyes lost some of their apprehension; regarded me with what I took to be cold curiosity. "Why would you have done that?"

"I knew she'd been waiting outside your apartment. You ran out to get away from her, didn't you?"

"Yes. I was watching for—somebody else, and saw her. She followed me. I'm sure she must have followed me. I tried to lose her."

"Why would Eve want to kill you, Lorry?"

The elevator groaned to a stop and I opened the door. The girl looked at me very steadily for a moment before she stepped out.

"Why? Because she *has to!*" Her expression suggested I should have known anything so obvious. "You see, I'm the only person who knows she shot her husband."

"I think we'd better go in and talk this over."

21

I decided, as we walked into the living room, that I'd better accept Lorry's statement as the truth—at least for the moment. Huck Trask's unhappy doubts about his wife reinforced my belief. If she had been the author of Johnny's apparently foolproof murder, then things had suddenly gone wrong; she would be tough to handle. She would have followed Lorry to see if she went to the police or to me, and a desperate Eve was perfectly capable of barging in and raising some very serious hell.

I pulled the shades down carefully and got my frightened visitor settled on the couch—a small, cowering heap. I wondered if she could find the courage to sit there alone for five minutes; asked her.

"Oh—it would be awful. Why must I stay here alone?"

"I want to make sure Eve Trask isn't watching the windows. I'll be right by the building all the time. If she's coming in I want to know it—don't you?"

"Yes. I would want to know that—"

"I won't be gone more than three or four minutes at the most. If anything frightens you, you can lock yourself in the office—it's through the kitchen."

"I guess I'll be all right. Please don't be long."

I turned off all the lights except the small reading lamp near Lorry, got my hat, and went out into the hall. The elevator was still standing at the floor. There was no one in the hall or on the stairway as I went down. I had half a thought about looking on the landing above, but didn't bother to go back.

The late-evening wanderers were ambling around the street as usual. I didn't see Eve among them and it didn't make much difference. I wanted her to see me if she was around. I walked at a businesslike pace to the restaurant and went in. Although I hadn't eaten there often, they knew me from my recent cat hunt when I'd prowled their cellar. Nobody paid much attention to me in the after-theater clatter, and I went through to the back.

The chef said, "Still looking for your cat?"

"Yeah. Mind if I go through? I thought I heard her a while ago."

"Help yourself."

The alley was dark and deserted. I took a careful look around and hurried through to the intersecting alley and out into Forty-eighth, some distance below. A quick duck across the street landed me near the rear entrance of my apartment house, and I went in.

If Eve had been watching, she'd have me placed in the restaurant. Unless she went in, she couldn't know I wasn't there. I went through to the stairway and up from the empty lobby. There was no sound as I stood at my door. Someone had gone in—or come out. The door had not been securely closed. I pushed it open an inch or two. There was no light whatever in the apartment.

It was strictly a spot where angels fear to tread, and I didn't do any rushing in. I considered calling out, but was afraid I'd start something. A deploying movement to the left flank seemed indicated, and I moved carefully down the hall to the office door, unlocked it noiselessly, and pushed it slightly open. The waiting room was still reminiscent of the morning's visitors, and no air current suggested an open door any place.

I listened at the entrance to the consultation room—closed, now, but without a lockable latch. There was no sound. There were a lot of possibilities. Lorry could have simply beat it—or was sitting in there in the dark for some reason, with the door open. Or Eve could be waiting somewhere in the apartment for her—and/or me. It wasn't comfortable.

To turn on a light would give the stalker an open invitation to make trouble. I thought dismally of the damned gun I'd left on the mantel. It probably wouldn't be there now.

I turned the knob slowly and pulled the door open a little at a time. It squeaks at about three quarters of the way, and I avoided swinging it that far. A dim glare from the window profiled my desk and chairs. No one in the room. I moved forward and found the kitchen entrance closed. No light showed under it. I touched the knob—

The telephone startled me—buzzed in the office and rang dimly beyond in the bedroom. It rang four times before I made up my mind to answer it. I caught the interval between the fifth and sixth ring and picked up the instrument—hoping that anyone in the apartment would think the caller had given it up. I said, "Yes." Quick and low.

"Doc?"

"Yes. Make it quick and don't make me talk."

"This is Johnson. You in trouble?"

I waited.

"I'll be right over, Doc—but listen; something come back to me that I can't get out of my head. I'll make it fast, but hang up if you want me there right now."

I waited.

"O.K. When I was standing in the alley watching for Mrs. Trask to get out of her car, somebody back at the other end opened a trash can and closed it again. I couldn't see the person, but, as I remember it, whoever it was seemed to be trying to make as little noise as possible. It was right at the time the Mallo girl would have been sneaking out. Could she have thrown something in there—like the gun? If it sounds no good, just hang up."

The gun was in the hands of the police, Trask's envelope was locked in my file, and Mickey's betting slip was of no further use since there was plenty of other evidence of the deal. I had no idea what Lorry could have hidden, but if she had stopped to get rid of something under that much pressure, it had to be important.

I waited.

"I'll go through that can if you don't need me there for a while. If you want me to, you can hang up, and I'll be on my way."

I hung up. A fraction of a second later the telephone box made a small click—familiar because it always happens when the extension is hung up in the bedroom. It had been a three-cornered conversation, and the third party had me located. If it had been the badly scared Lorry, she'd be locked in and, as witnessed by the open hall door, Eve Trask would be waiting in the living room for something to break. I would have gambled that she had my gun in her hand if she hadn't brought one of her own. Maybe the women each had one. A distinctly unpleasant thought.

I quietly pulled down the window shade to avoid light behind me and went to the kitchen door. I'd just gotten it open a few inches when somebody spoke in the darkness beyond. It was Eve Trask's voice, and definitely the gun-in-hand one.

"All right, come out. I heard you moving in there."

I almost spoke before I realized she wasn't talking to me; heard her rattle the knob of the bedroom door. No response from inside.

"Listen, Red; you've done all the damage you can do—you're washed up. Through." I decided to listen too. As long as Lorry kept the door locked she was reasonably safe. "For three years you and Johnny Mallo have made my life unbearable—but that's over. Now Johnny's dead and his blood-money partner is in the hospital with a bullet in his head. You're next, Red, and you signed your own warrant twice"—I heard the elevator click but refused to move. I must have left the door open. The woman paid no attention to it, or didn't hear it—"once, a long time ago, when you asked me how I kept my figure, and once, today, when you showed up outside my husband's office building. It was stupid of me not to remember you'd know about the Nembutal. I'm not being stupid any more. *I'm coming in to get you.*"

The terrible intensity of the woman's voice shut out the noises from the street, the hammering of my heart, and the steady tread of a man's feet which must have been sounding on the stairway outside. But it didn't shut out Lorry Mallo's muffled cry, "Don't touch that door, Eve! Doc Connor's right behind you. He's just waiting for you to—"

"Doc Connor doesn't even know you're here—he couldn't. He's eating in the restaurant across the street. For once you haven't got a man to take care of you, you cheap punk." The doorknob rattled roughly.

Lorry screamed. "No! Shoot her, Doc! Get her! Now you know it's true about her. She's going to break down the door!"

Then silence. I heard the footsteps on the stairs. Eddie Marsh or Elegant. I waited to call out a warning. Eve spoke very softly. If she heard the man outside, she paid no attention.

"Doc?"

It seemed no time to invite a shot in my direction. Either Marsh or Johnson would be armed. I kept quiet.

The steps were in the hall then. I sensed that the woman had moved away from the door—deeper into the room. I kept hoping to hear the dial of Lorry's telephone. I was needed where I was and couldn't use the extension. There was a sudden sharp rap at the hall door, though I'd left it open. Eddie wouldn't have knocked.

"Connor!" A man's voice—familiar. "I say, Connor! Are you inside?"

I called out. "Pack?"

"Yes. Put on a light. Mrs. Mallo called me—"

"Pack! Listen! Stay where you are and don't touch the lights. Eve Trask is somewhere in the room with a gun."

Silence for a moment, then I heard the Trask woman laugh. I've heard a couple of other people laugh under unbearable pressure. There's nothing funny about it. There was a quick, light series of steps away from me and toward the hall door.

I hollered, "Look out, Pack!" Then the lights went on and I ducked aside. I heard a key grind in a lock. It could have been the bedroom. I blinked around the corner and looked into the living room. Eve was standing by the light switch holding out her empty hands, smiling.

"I haven't got any gun."

The bedroom door swung wide. Lorry stood there. *"I have!"*

She stared squint-eyed but steady into the bright room. My automatic was stuck out in front of her.

Pack had committed himself inside—stood there—said, "Lorry! Are you all right?"

"Shut up, Ralph! Get out of that doorway."

Pack stood aside and watched her with staring eyes as she moved cautiously toward the hall. I caught a glimpse of the hammer on my gun. It was cocked. Lorry was playing for keeps. She circled around and ended up facing us from the door, her back to the hall.

Eve said, "You won't get away with it, Red—I can—"

The girl spat, "Keep quiet, Eve! Next time you open your mouth I'll start shooting." Her mouth made a hard scarlet rectangle. "For those clumsy piano legs of yours, Corky, you've always tried so hard to reduce."

I cut in. "Take it easy, Lorry—we can't settle anything—" I guess I took a step forward because she turned the gun sharply at my belly.

"I'm doing the talking for everybody right now, Doc—you do the listening. I don't like holding a gun on you and Ralph, but I've got no choice. You both heard this woman threaten to kill me, and neither of you made a move. You've both tried to be helpful, but as detectives you stink. I can't take a chance."

Pack seemed hurt. "I'm sure the man I employed through Fenner—"

"Don't make me laugh. The guy's working for Doc—trying to prove me guilty of something. You're not very bright, Pack. Now keep your mouth shut and go over beside the night-club beauty there." Pack looked pretty dazed. "Goddammit, *move!*"

He moved; stood beside Eve looking dopey.

"All right, Doc, you've heard this woman's confession. She's a killer and she's dangerous. She—"

Eve almost yelled. *"My what?* Why, you dirty—"

The redheaded girl did yell. "Do I have to shoot you?"

I said, "Better let her talk, Eve."

"Doc, she killed my husband because she'd been in love with him for years, and because he didn't want any part of her. I thought he did until I learned from Lieutenant Marsh how she'd tricked him out of a lot of money."

I silently damned Eddie, said, "Why would she have shot Huck, Lorry?"

"She had to. Huck Trask knew how she killed Johnny. Ask Ralph Pack."

I looked at the physician standing there with a very unhappy face hanging out. "What about it?"

"Trask called me this morning; asked about some jockey he'd known. He said the boy had been given a prescription for reducing—one I'd never suggest, certainly—amphetamine to check the appetite and nightly doses of Nembutal to overcome the restlessness conditioned by the Benzedrine. He'd forgotten the names of the drugs, but apparently knew the effect."

"Did he suggest that, in combination with nightly sweat baths, a course like that might be dangerous?"

The guy was flustered. "Not only that. He asked me if I thought it could have caused Mallo's death!"

"So you called Lorry to ask if Johnny might have taken a barbiturate?"

"Yes—of course. There seemed no reason to be suspicious. I didn't hear about Trask until—"

Lorry snapped, "I can't take this much longer, Doc—I'll blow my top. Go into the bedroom and call your friend Marsh, will you?"

The tension went out of me. I suddenly felt sorry for Huck Trask. His heartbreaking "It couldn't have been Eve. She couldn't have done this to me," cramped my throat. I went into the bedroom and picked up the phone. I could see the tableau outside—unmoving and silent.

I tried Eddie at home. No answer. He would still be at the precinct. I called there, and the sergeant said he was interviewing a suspect—that he'd get him to the phone.

Outside, Lorry Mallo stood almost in the shadow of the hall. The light from the room showed only her white face and the extended gun. She was alert, listening.

"Marsh."

"This is Doc, Eddie. Get up to my place on the double, will you?"

"What you got?"

"The works. Come on!"

"Right. I'll bring young Mallo." I watched the face in the doorway harden, the gun move. Eve stood poised, tense like a runner ready to break. "He's been doing some talking. The kid got the gun from Mrs. Mallo—" Something was about to happen outside. Lorry took half a step forward. The light described her whole figure. "She told him that it was—"

Then I knew the girl was going to shoot. I hollered, "Get going! I've got trouble!" I dropped the phone, and slammed out of the bedroom. Pack was frozen to the floor. Eve Trask jumped forward, her hand thrown up in front of her.

Lorry Mallo screamed, twisted her body sideways, clawed at her back. The gun crashed, spit orange flame, and slid along the floor. I moved in fast, stopped dead in my tracks as I got close to the screaming woman.

Over her shoulder I saw a pair of blazing blue eyes in a black face.

Sauki-no-no had come home!

22

I grabbed Lorry and hung on. The cat streaked across the floor and disappeared into the bedroom. I yelled to Pack.

"Lock her in, quick!"

He promptly started to wrestle with Eve, who shoved him halfway across the room. "No! The cat! Close the bedroom door before she gets out again."

All of which colloquy cost me some painful and indelicate swats. The clawing fury in my arms was inching me toward the stairway. I slammed her back into the room and jumped after her. She headed straight for Eve Trask, hysterical, screaming. Pack ran forward from shutting the door, then stood, transfixed, at the sight of his ideal woman on a rampage.

A police siren whined into Forty-eighth Street, and rubber howled against the pavement.

Lorry rushed at her target full on. The big blonde went up on her toes and did a very fancy piece of footwork—a fast shift to the left—and dropped in as neat a right cross as you'll see outside the Garden. La Mallo hit the deck and stayed there.

Pack said, "Oh! You've hurt her!"

Eve said, "Are you kidding?"

I said, "Nice shot, champ." I put the gun in my coat pocket and went over to Eve. Pack was on his knees beside Lorry. "You don't look too good, Corky."

She tried a grin that didn't work out. "I've got news for you, Doc. I'm going to pass out."

While I was boosting her up in my arms I heard a lot of feet pounding on the stairway. The Marines were a little late. Eddie boomed in with his gun ahead of him. I saw Mickey Mallo with a uniformed cop beside him.

Marsh laughed and put up his gun. I was staggering toward the couch with Eve. As I turned to put her down, I saw Pack parading behind with his arms full of very limp woman. I told him the ward was full and to take his patient some place else.

Eddie said, "Well I'll be damned!" He walked into the room. "A Roman orgy or I never read *Quo Vadis!* Want us to wait in the hall, Doc?"

The big lug makes me sore as hell sometimes. "No, dammit, either haul these people off to the station house or lock the Mallo girl up some place. I've got enough of her for the moment." I put Eve down and looked at Pack. He was still standing there with his droopy load. "Give her to Marsh, Pack. We'll lock her up."

The man stared at me sadly and sighed. "Perhaps we'd better, Doctor."

Eddie took Lorry into the bedroom and dumped her. "Hey, Doc! Your cat's back! What do you know? She remembered me and jumped on my shoulder!"

I went in and carted Sauki-no-no off to the kitchen, poured her some canned milk. When I got back, Eddie was changing the key to the outside of the bedroom door and everybody was standing around. Eve Trask was up again, fixing her hair. The uniformed cop was posted in the outer doorway. Mickey Mallo was frowning, puzzled.

Marsh said, "All right, Doc, what's this about?"

"The Mallo girl was going to hang everything on Mrs. Trask and then dig up a reason to shoot her—in self-defense. She damned near did it, at that. It was pretty convincing."

Eve said, "I'll say it was. God, I'm glad it came off that way though! I wasn't sure until this afternoon that my husband hadn't gone off his chump and killed Johnny—just when we were free from him for good." She shook her head. "I knew Huck had heard my doctor's warning about the sweat baths and sleeping pills. We didn't dare talk about it, but we both knew how Johnny had died from the time it happened. It was dreadful."

I said, "Huck thought you'd done it, Eve." I didn't have the heart not to add, "Until he was shot, of course."

"Poor Huck! He was always a little jealous of Johnny—even though I had learned to hate the man. Johnny was always narrow and mean-minded—right to the last. When Huck paid him off Friday night, he claimed the contract was at his lawyer's office. I knew he wouldn't trust anybody with it, and I went to his apartment house and waited for him—even followed him upstairs and begged him for it—"

Eddie spoke up. "Mallo had canceled it, Mrs. Trask. He'd intended to give it back."

"I suppose he did—it was just that he couldn't do anything any way but nastily. He laughed at me, and I went home."

One by one, everybody sat down except the cop at the door. I said, "I was stupid not to put things together right. I got tangled up in a lot of stuff that didn't count—outsmarted myself."

Eddie said, "You always do. Like what, this time?"

"Like Lorry Mallo's figure, for instance—"

Marsh laughed. "The male climacteric can account for some weird lapses."

"Lorry's concern for her figure keyed the whole thing. The first night I ever saw Mallo's reducing room, I stood there and looked at evidence that she had been there after Johnny had started his bath—that she had been absolutely callous to the fact that her husband was dead or dying in that cabinet. It could have been no one else concerned. I stood there and looked at it—and didn't see it."

Eddie glowered at me. "What's all this? Why didn't you—"

"Because I didn't know, then, what I was looking at. Pack will remember. The scales were set a full two inches to the right—heavier, that is—of any weight Johnny or Mickey could possibly have brought to bear. Two inches is eight pounds. The balance was left at one eighteen or nineteen—too light by far for the Trasks or Pack! I'll gamble that's Lorry Mallo's weight— give or take a pound. There's a scale in the office if you—"

"Hell, Doc! That isn't evidence. Mallo could have knocked the balance with his arm. He needn't have weighed at all before he started his bath."

Mickey said, "That don't make sense. How would a rider know how long to stay in if he didn't know how much he weighed?" Everybody looked at him, and he stared at the bedroom door. "I—didn't think it could've been—like you say. But—" He looked like he was about to cry.

I said, "She's bad, Mick. You'd better get that through your head. She put you up to the Nautilus fix, didn't she?"

He looked at the floor; scuffed his feet. Pack made a sound in his throat. "Yeah. She said it was her only chance to get free. Johnny was awful close with us—we couldn't either of us get out from under ever. When Ralph Pack turned me down, Lorry put everything she had on the horse—money she'd been scrambling for for a couple of years."

Eddie said, "And she turned the gun over to you today. She told you Eve Trask had borrowed it, shot her husband with it, then sneaked in, and planted it back in the apartment."

The boy said nothing. I asked him what he'd been doing in Mallo's apartment Monday night.

"You know already, Doc. I saw Huck pay Johnny a lot of money and I knew Lorry didn't know about it. I wanted to get it for her before the Trasks took it back. The apartment was full of people on Saturday and Sunday."

Eve grinned a little. "I guess you know why I was nosing around, Doc."

"Yes. I've got the contract—courtesy of Mickey, here." Eddie Marsh looked worried, impatient. He got up and paced around. "Listen, Doc, I've got that woman penned up in there with nothing solid against her but a weapon. All this chat doesn't get us anywhere." The cop in the door moved aside, said something under his breath, and Elegant Johnson came in carrying some large metal object hanging from a string. Marsh was still walking with his back turned. "Weights on a scale! I need something with some weight *to* it."

Eve was looking at Johnson, her mouth hanging open. She whooped, coughed out, "So did I!" Then she practically had hysterics.

Elegant Johnson looked at her with a blank face. "What did I do?"

The thing he was dangling was a chrome water jug, the string through the handle, obviously to preserve possible prints. "You find that—where you said, Elegant?"

"Yeah. Shoved down under some stuff."

I turned to Mickey. "Ever see that before, Mick?"

"It was theirs—Johnny's."

Pack put in, "I've seen it often at the Mallos'. Mrs. Mallo kept it on her—bed table—" Then he took his foot out of his mouth and added a pompous, "I often visited the young people professionally."

Eve howled again. I said, "What the hell's the matter with you?"

She wiped her eyes. "The lieutenant wanted something with some weight to it. Well, there it is. That is the convenient object I defended myself with the night I—mistook you for a burglar."

Eddie Marsh took the bottle from Elegant. "So what's it mean to me?"

If he'd held his breath thirty seconds he wouldn't have asked. As it was, I found myself getting very happy. "It wraps up the case for you, pal. It lets Lorry Mallo be in Long Island while her husband is being murdered. Thoughtful little wife leaves her man's hot, sweet chocolate in the thermos jug—complete with four grains of Nembutal. You're sure to find spectroscopic evidence of the drug. It was a fairly strong solution in a gummy substance. It'll stick in the seams, even with a quick rinsing. Five'll get you ten it's good for a confession, anyway."

The big cop looked a little relieved. "That makes more sense than anything you've said yet." He frowned. "We'll see." He frowned more. "By God, Doc, you can take a simple job of husband killing and fog it up so badly that nobody in his right mind can recognize it." He walked over to the bedroom door. "I don't know why I ever listen to you!"

"I turned up with your good, solid evidence, didn't I?" The lug turned the key and looked over his shoulder. "Hell! Some woman *would* have to hit you over the head with it!"

He opened the door, said, "Come on, Lorry."

The Ohio operator tried to give me a "don't answer," and I kept her ringing. Finally Katie croaked on and accused me of being drunk.

"I'm not at all, darling. I haven't had a drink since—"

Good Lord! I *hadn't,* either!

"Since when? And why are you calling me at four in the morning? Has something happened?"

"Everything's all right now. You see, Sauki-no-no's back. I was frantically worried—"

"Jimmy! Sauki-no-no's back from *where?* Is she all right?"

"Why—yes. She's perfectly all right—I mean physically. You see she slipped—"

"How did she slip? Cats don't slip. Send for Dr. Severance at once if there's something wrong with her."

"Don't pick me up so fast, will you? The cat slipped out of the building and played around with another cat in the alley for—quite a while."

"Well, why do you worry about that now that she's back? She's been inoculated against distemper, feline enteritis, and—"

"She hasn't been inoculated against what I was worrying about—tom cats, I mean. The social implications are— What's so damned funny?"

"But she has, Jimmy darling! If you'd ever bothered to brush her belly, you'd have known. It shows. You're certainly not very observing."

I'm not—am I?

Print-on-demand titles available at
CoachwhipBooks.com

Ebook titles available at
Coachwhip.com

ODDS-ON MURDER

JACK DOLPH

murder is mutuel

JACK DOLPH

Jack Dolph

MURDER MAKES THE MARE GO

JACK DOLPH

DEAD ANGEL

A.M. JAUSS

MURDER ENDS
THE SONG

ALFRED MEYERS

MURDER
A LA
MODE

ELEANORE
KELLY
SELLARS

CLASSIC RED BADGE PRIZE MYSTERY

MURDER IN
MALAYA

FATAL SHADOWS

*DEATH OVER
HER SHOULDER*

DOROTHY
COLE
MEADE

MURDER
IN A WALLED TOWN

KATHERINE WOODS

DRESSED
TO KILL

Emma Lou Jetta

MURDER
ON THE
FACE OF IT

Emma Lou Jetta

MURDER IN STYLE

Emma Lou Jetta

THE MUMMY CASE MYSTERY

DERMOT MORRAH

VIRGINIA RATH

DEATH AT
DAYTON'S FOLLY

MURDER ON
THE DAY OF
JUDGMENT

VIRGINIA RATH

VIRGINIA RATH

THE ANGER
OF THE BELLS

MURDER

with a theme song

VIRGINIA RATH

THE HEX MURDER

Alexander Williams

MURDER TAKES
THE VEIL

MURDER AT
ST. DENNIS

SISTER SIMON'S
MURDER CASE

THE MARGARET ANN HUBBARD
MYSTERY OMNIBUS

THE PHILOSOPHER'S
MURDER CASE

JACK R. CRAWFORD